Kate & Frida

Kate & Frida

*A Novel of Friendship,
Food, and Books*

Kim Fay

G. P. Putnam's Sons
New York

PUTNAM
— EST. 1838 —

G. P. PUTNAM'S SONS
Publishers Since 1838
An imprint of Penguin Random House LLC
penguinrandomhouse.com

Library of Congress Cataloging-in-Publication Data

Names: Fay, Kim, author.
Title: Kate & Frida : a novel of friendship, food, and books / by Kim Fay.
Other titles: Kate and Frida
Description: New York : G. P. Putnam's Sons, 2025.
Identifiers: LCCN 2024029473 (print) | LCCN 2024029474 (ebook) |
ISBN 9780593852385 (hardcover) | ISBN 9780593852392 (epub)
Subjects: LCSH: Friendship—Fiction. | Bookstores—Fiction. | LCGFT: Novels.
Classification: LCC PS3606.A9524 K38 2025 (print) |
LCC PS3606.A9524 (ebook) | DDC 813/.6—dc23/eng/20240628
LC record available at https://lccn.loc.gov/2024029473
LC ebook record available at https://lccn.loc.gov/2024029474

Printed in the United States of America
1st Printing

Book design by Laura K. Corless
Title page and part opener illustrations by Christie Kwan

for Woodrow "Buck" Ethier (1912–1992)

for Kurt (1964–2005) and Roy (1965–2007)

& for all of us tender dreamers
at the Elliott Bay Book Company
during those precious years before the internet changed
everything

PART ONE

Youth is wholly experimental. The essence and charm of that unquiet and delightful epoch is ignorance of self as well as ignorance of life.

—Robert Louis Stevenson, *Across the Plains*

FRIDA RODRIGUEZ ... EN ROUTE

October 2, 1991
Paris, France

Bonjour Puget Sound Book Company!

Greetings from my midnight view at Hôtel La Louisiane. Ivory moonlight glinting off zinc rooftops. An autumn chill in the air and me at my desk – cocooned in a baggy sweater à la Julie Christie in <u>Doctor Zhivago</u> – as I continue to hunt for a book. Naturally! Why else would I be writing to you? I spent the whole day with my new pal Kirby scouring the City of Lights. Of course we hit the venerable Shakespeare and Company and gave Village Voice a chance and the bookstalls too – only to discover that this magnifique metropolis is awash in macho old Hemingway but good luck finding his better half.

I need Martha Gellhorn's <u>The Face of War</u>!

Normally I'd order from my beloved Vroman's in L.A. but Kirby won our contest for finding to-die-for moules marinières. Now I have to do something he tells me to do and he's telling me to order Martha from you – we've been debating bookstores for almost a week and he claims you're #1. He's from Seattle – clearly biased – no offense. That said, I'm a card-carrying bookstore addict and I intend to try as many as I can before I die. I've been keeping a list since I was six and I can't wait to add you to it.

I'm enclosing a traveler's check. It should be enough to splurge for air mail. See address below.

Thank you and au revoir!

Frida Rodriguez

Hôtel La Louisiane

60 rue de Seine

75006 Paris, France

P.S. Sorry about the splotches. My éclair sprung a leak!

THE PUGET SOUND BOOK COMPANY

101 South Main Street   Seattle, WA 98104

10/14/91

Dear Frida,

My name is Kate Fair. I'm not the one who opened your letter, but I was told I'm the only person here who's perky enough to respond to you. It's not midnight (the store closes at eleven), and I don't have romantic rooftop views, but it's nice here at night, too. I'm at the information desk, which is actually two big old desks facing each other on a low platform in the middle of the store. When it gets really quiet like now, it feels like I walked through the wardrobe into Narnia, but instead of magical creatures I find magical books in big quiet caverns with creaking wood floors and soaring brick ceilings. It smells homey like my Bumpa's trailer because there's a café in the basement with coffee brewing all the time. We can have as much as we want for free.

Confession: When <u>The Face of War</u> arrived I was just going to peek at the first few pages, but I couldn't put it down. Talk about ~~awesome~~ eye-opening. My brain is jittering with wars I've never even heard about. I was careful, but I guess it's technically a used book now. I gave you my employee discount to make up for it and hopefully keep the store from losing #1 status with your friend Kirby.

How ~~awesome~~ exciting to live in Paris. When I was in junior high I had a poster of the Eiffel Tower on my wall. I planned to live in a garret in Montmartre. Obviously that didn't happen. How did you end up in France? Where are you en route to? How many moules marinières did you have to eat to find to-die-for? How many bookstores have you been to? (I'm a bookstore addict, too. I just looked up Shakespeare and Company in a Time Out guidebook in our travel section and added it to my wish list.) Sorry for all the questions. I hope you don't mind. If you do, don't feel like you have to answer.

If you need more books, I promise I won't read them first. Your credit is on your receipt.

Sincerely,

Kate

FRIDA RODRIGUEZ ... EN ROUTE

October 30, 1991
Paris, France

Bonjour Perky Kate!

I come to you once again from midnight and my rooftop view. Sometimes I still can't believe I'm in Paris – that's why I end up wide awake half the night waiting for dawn so I can go out and make more discoveries. It's not like L.A. where you need a car to go everywhere – it's fun to walk here. Today Kirby and I accidentally stumbled on one of those risqué art films at Le Champo – no need for subtitles there! – followed by overindulgence at a kebab shop in the Saint-Michel district. And the Metro! It's like the transporter in <u>Star Trek</u> – beam me to the Moulin Rouge, Scotty! Tomorrow we're going to decide whether or not we approve of the Louvre Pyramid and the Centre Pompidou.

Merci for the book and the discount – no biggie about reading Martha before you sent her. I'm sitting here on my bed with a croissant and a glass of Beaujolais and I've already spilled wine on the cover and there's butter soaked through the introduction. No one does butter like the French – parfait!

So what's Frida Rodriguez doing in Paris besides not sleeping? She's en route to her future! It started last year when I read that <u>Time</u> article about twentysomethings. The part about mass apathy got to me and when that writer called us the New Petulants I had an epiphany. Not even twenty-five and I was on my fourth writing job – and I'd whined about every one of them! Even worse, the aforementioned fourth job was with <u>West Coast Commerce</u> disguising advertorials as financial news. I blame that one on my fleeting Ayn Rand phase in college. By the way – "Greed is good" is the stupidest thing a person can say!

Anyway I'm thinking – seriously Frida! Why'd you even bother getting a journalism degree? That's when it hit me. Get out of L.A. and pursue my dream of writing something meaningful. So I saved up my money and came to Paris – just like Martha back in her day – to see the world and be close to all the history in the making around here. Is this letter sounding like the unabridged version of a personal ad in the back of the <u>L.A. Times</u>? Single brownish-whitish girl, nonsmoking, loves kebabs and long walks on the beach, tired of yuppies and New Petulance and wants to do something of consequence before she wakes up one day and she's thirty and it's too late!

How's that for a slapdash answer to your questions? My problem is I can type on my mom's old très chic portable Hermes Rocket faster than I can think. Well one of my problems. To spend that credit – what are you reading right now that you absolutely <u>LOVE</u>? Surprise me! I play this game with my dad when we go to bookstores. We tell them a little about ourselves and then rate the store by the surprise.

Au revoir!
Frida

P.S. Nothing wrong with being Perky Peggy. I'll take it over Gloomy Gertie any day.

P.S. Deux. Adding Paris, I've been to thirty-six different bookstores in my life so far, mostly in L.A. and Mexico.

P.S. Trois. I almost forgot to explain the moules marinières competition. Fellow American Kirby Olsson is on an exchange from the University of Washington at l'École nationale supérieure d'architecture de Paris-Belleville – how's that for a mouthful! He lives here at the hotel too and I discovered he's a Fellow Glutton. I told him about some disappointing moules marinières I had and he said he heard where to get good ones but it turned out they were just decent and that set off our contest. We each chose five restaurants and may the best moules marinières win! Kirby hit on to-die-for at Chez Lisette – a cozy bistro a few blocks from the hotel with a view of the Seine to boot – and that is how I wound up ordering Martha from his favorite bookstore. You're officially added to my list but I'll wait to rate you until I receive my surprise. No pressure!

11/15/91

Dear Frida,

Paris sounds ~~awesome~~ divine. I ~~totally~~ admire you for follow-ing your dream. I'm pretty much trying to do that, too. My dad and I have a thing for bookstores like you and your dad, and when I was growing up he'd do these special daughter days for my little sis, Franny, and me. Every year we got to come to Seattle with him by ourselves for a Seahawks game. Before heading to the Kingdome we'd walk around Pioneer Square. We always visited this one little bookshop. I remember thinking how ~~awesome~~ in-credible it would be to work there someday. The little bookshop grew up, and guess what? I'm working in it right now.

Not that it feels like work. I love it, especially when I manage to help a customer find what they want. A little while ago a man came up, and this is how he described the book he was looking for. "It has bright colors on the cover, and I think the word be-trayal is in the title, or maybe not, but it's about South Africa or maybe South America." That's why I spend so much time brows-ing covers and titles in different sections. This kind of thing hap-

pens a lot. It was my own private victory to figure out he wanted
My Traitor's Heart.

Confession: When I asked you about the moules marinières
competition, I didn't know what moules marinières were. I went
up to Campagne (this French restaurant in Pike Place Market) to
see if I could try them, and when asked about them, I was ~~totally~~
embarrassed. Moules are mussels. I should know that because (a)
I took two years of French in high school and (b) Seattle serves
more than its fair share of mussels. The restaurant was ~~way too
Thurston Howell the 3rd~~ too lavish for an impoverished bookseller, so I walked down to Ivar's and got my favorite fried clam
strips and chips. I sat on the pier and watched the ferries glide out
to the islands. People think it's just rain and gray skies in Seattle,
but we get these flawless days. The bay was dark blue satin, and
whitecaps danced with silver sunlight. In the distance, the Olympic Mountains looked like glaciers floating in the sky. It was parfait, as you say.

I've been agonizing over your surprise. There are so many
books to choose from, and what if I ~~totally~~ blow it? I finally
picked Moon Tiger by Penelope Lively. (It's fiction. I hope you're
okay with that.) It's so exceptional I gave myself a goal to hand-
sell a hundred copies in a single month. Last month I sold eighty-
nine. Now I've already sold sixty-eight and it's only halfway
through November. Selling you a copy gets me closer, but that's
not why I picked it. The main character, Claudia, is a war correspondent in Egypt during WWII, and the book is about how she
reflects back on her life. I thought you'd like that. Plus it made

my brain jitter. (My brain jitters a lot these days.) All those different points of view. I mean, who knew you could switch back and forth between first person and third person for the same character? Not me when I wrote my novel.

Sincerely,

Kate

P.S. How long did it take you to save up enough money to live in Paris?

Frida Rodriguez ... En Route

November 26, 1991
Paris, France

Perky Kate,

It's not midnight and I'm not in my hotel room. What better place to finish reading Martha Gellhorn than a window seat at the storied and oh so literary Café de Flore while sipping chocolat chaud poured out of a little silver teapot to keep the cold at bay? Martha is my new heroine! How did she write with a clear head about such grim situations? When I got to the section about Dachau I cried. Do you think Martha ever cried? I'm trying to figure out how she makes you feel the horror you're supposed to feel about things like that without her own emotions spilling all over the place. That's great journalism!

Friends from school say I should do TV news because I have such a big personality but I think it's the words that will last. I'm reading Martha's words all these years later in the very café where she once sat and they're still an emotional gut punch. People aren't going to dig back through old videocassettes to watch CNN clips about Desert Storm. How would they even do it? But words – wordswordswords – wow! Do you see that? The pen and the sword!

I socked away money for almost a year but unfortunately not enough to live here <u>and</u> indulge in cheese daily without working. I have a part-time job cleaning up English documents for a translation company. Not ideal but my choices were limited through the visa program I used. At least they pay by the project – they weren't prepared for how fast I can type – between that and my savings I can afford to base myself here. So much is happening in this part of the world. Berlin's reunited, the Soviet Union's breaking up, Yugoslavia's heating up. I'm trying to learn as much as possible while I figure out a way to get someone to hire me to cover one of the wars that keep breaking out.

Wow! Did you soak your stationery in truth serum? Besides Kirby you're the first person I've told why I'm really here. My parents think I'm taking a break to eat Camembert and soul search and I don't want any of my old friends accidentally mentioning it to them – no need for parental freak-outs until I'm actually in a war zone. They're taking it hard enough that I'm staying here for Christmas but if my plan works out there will be times when I'm in the thick of it and can't come home so I figure this is good practice even if they don't know it. I was worried I'd be lonely spending the holidays away even though I'm the independent type but Kirby said he'll take me to the Christmas markets. We plan to drink buckets of vin chaud and gorge on local delicacies. No roasted chestnuts for me – grainy mush nuggets – but the French make a crème caramel that will knock your socks off and I can't get enough raclette. Whoever came up with the idea of scraping melted cheese over bread and salami should be given a Nobel. I hope it snows!

I'm sending another traveler's check. Keep the War Journo Dames coming and I'll take another book you LOVE. Bravo on the surprise! Boy oh boy did <u>Moon Tiger</u> speak to me. It's like you knew exactly what I need to read right now. I love how the main character Claudia is her own woman. She doesn't second-guess herself or do anything because she thinks other people think she should. And when she said "I've grown old with this century; there's not much left of either of us. The century of war. All history, of course, is the history of wars, but this hundred years has excelled itself." Isn't that the truth! That's why I need to use my journo degree for something more important than stock trends.

Now what about you? Why is Kate the Bookseller's brain always jittering? Why didn't she send me her novel? Inquiring minds want to know. I'm the one who's impressed! I could never write anything that long. I have the attention span of a goldfish on NoDoz – or one zap of a TV dial as that dumb <u>Time</u> article says.
Au revoir,
Frida

P.S. I hope you sell those hundred copies of <u>Moon Tiger</u>!

12/7/91

Dear Frida,

I hope you can read my scrawl. I'm wearing a pair of fingerless gloves, not to mention long johns under a flannel shirt <u>and</u> a sweater, but my hands are still cramped with cold. I'm so relieved you like <u>Moon Tiger</u>. I've been working hard to read all kinds of books so I can recommend what a person will want to read and not just what I want them to read.

I'm really honored you told me you want to write about wars. Your secret is safe in Seattle. I wish my secret was as interesting as yours. The reason I didn't send you my novel is because it didn't get published. I finished it after I graduated from college, and then I got an agent. An ~~awesome~~ reputable Boston publisher called Little, Brown was interested, but the editor wanted some changes. She told me I needed to get closer to the heart of my character's motivation, but every time I gave her a revision, she said I was further away.

It was about a young woman from a small town who travels around the world trying to learn as much as she can about life, but the more she learns the more she discovers how much she still doesn't know. My editor had been to the Galápagos and New Zealand, and she said I ~~nailed~~ have an authentic grasp of those places. I guess the character didn't feel real. The confusing thing is I've never been out of the U.S. except to Canada. I just used Lonely Planet guides. But the character is me. How can she not feel real if she's me?

I mean, the story was basically inspired by my own life. I've been into books since before I can remember. My mom says I'd sit and turn pages even before I could read, and I was reciting <u>Miss Twiggley's Tree</u> by heart with her when I was three. I read every single Time-Life book Bumpa gave us for Christmas. By the time I finished junior high I'd written half a dozen novels. Mostly mysteries and romances since I was into Nancy Drew and Harlequins and <u>Love Story</u>, and I thought I was the most literate kid in my high school because I read <u>Gone with the Wind</u> twice. Then I got into college. Talk about a wake-up call. I remember this English class where the professor told us to rewrite one of our stories in the style of Virginia Woolf. Everyone was ~~totally~~ excited about doing stream of consciousness. I had no idea what they were talking about. It got worse every time the professor assigned another author I didn't know. I read as much as I could as fast as I could, but there was always more to read, which is how I got the idea for my novel.

I kind of wonder if it didn't work because I could never figure out how to get my character to the place where she finally knew all the things she needed to know. I was really stuck, and about a month ago my agent told me it's time to stop and maybe try something ~~totally~~ different. How depressing is that? Especially since I have no idea what I should write next. I keep reading popular books here at the store, and I'm definitely not a Tama Janowitz or Darcey Steinke. Even if I wanted to write a book like <u>Suicide Blonde</u>, which I don't, I couldn't. That first line about pink walls quivering like v – – – lips. No way. My co-worker Stella calls me a prude. She has wild auburn curls and is a total grunge chick in vintage dresses and Doc Martens. She reads edgy authors like John Fante and Oscar Wilde and thinks it's funny to ask me inappropriate questions because I turn red. This makes me worry, what if I write another book and no one wants to read it because all they're interested in is <u>American Psycho</u> and <u>Damage</u>?

The secret part is that I haven't told anyone at the store what happened because I was hoping when I got published everyone would take me seriously. The other day Dawn (she's one of my co-workers who calls me perky) actually told me to quit telling customers to have a nice day. I asked her, "What if I want them to?" That ~~totally~~ irritated her. And it's not just my personality that's different. They all know so much about literature. Like this other co-worker Sven. We're close to the same age, but the last time we worked at the front counter together, he was talking about Martin Heidegger like they're best friends. I just nodded and then snuck away and looked up who he was talking about.

Yikes! Sorry about rambling. I had no idea all that was going to flood out of my pen. I'll sign off now before I bore you to death.
Sincerely,
Kate

P.S. I almost sealed the envelope without explaining what I'm sending. I usually work the information desk at night with a guy named Roy. I told him about you. (I guess your secret's not so safe in Seattle, but he's trustworthy.) He adores British authors, and he says you have to read <u>Black Lamb and Grey Falcon</u> if you want to know about Yugoslavia. Rebecca West wasn't really a War Journo Dame, but Roy says she covered the Nuremberg Trials for <u>The New Yorker</u>. She seems like she's up your alley. (I'm glad I read Martha. I didn't have to pretend I knew what the Nuremberg Trials were and then go look them up in the encyclopedia at the library.)

P.P.S. I'm still figuring out your next Surprise Me book.

P.P.P.S. I sold 104 copies of <u>Moon Tiger</u> last month.

P.P.P.P.S. I can't stop thinking about what you wrote: "It's the words that will last." It's so true. You can count on books. Like Claudia says in <u>Moon Tiger</u>: "Fiction can seem more enduring than reality. Pierre on the field of battle, the Bennet girls at their sewing, Tess on the threshing machine – all these are nailed down for ever, on the page and in a million heads." I want to write something that's worth being nailed down forever.

FRIDA RODRIGUEZ ... EN ROUTE

December 21, 1991
Paris, France

Joyeux Noël Kate, although it might be Bonne Année by the time you get this letter!

First things first. Obviously Frida Rodriguez LOVES rambling! Ramble on Fair Bookseller. Ha! Are you fair Kate Fair?

I'm sorry about your novel not being published but you got an agent and a big publisher was interested. I bet that's more than most novelists get on their first try and who cares when you learned about Virginia Woolf – you know about her now <u>and</u> you know about Miss Twiggley. I bet no one at the bookstore can say that. To hell with quivering V lips! You'll never write a book that's worth being nailed down forever if you don't get yourself writing again. What do you love? Write about that!

I can't believe my moolah covered the postage for <u>Black Lamb</u> – it weighs ten tons – I have to read it propped on a pillow in my lap but tell your pal Roy beaucoup thanks. It's perfect timing. Kirby's studying the effect on a culture when its architecture is destroyed in a war, and he interviewed a couple foreign correspondents covering Yugoslavia. He's going to introduce me the next time they're back in Paris. Now I won't sound like a greenhorn when I pick their brains. Sarajevo? Why yes, says Well-Versed Frida leaning back in her chair at Chez Lisette and gazing thoughtfully into her wine glass – I believe the capital of Bosnia was founded by the Ottoman Empire in the 1400s. Indeed, say the foreign correspondents in response – how knowledgeable you are – you should come to the front lines with us. Daydream much Frida?

Speaking of Chez Lisette – Kirby started calling it our Cheers because we spend so much time there. I can't get enough of the house Beaujolais and Lisette's potatoes dauphinoise are out of this world. Forget any scalloped potatoes you ever ate at Thanksgiving. She throws in Jerusalem artichokes – that nutty flavor with the Gruyère – swoon! Especially in this weather.

You're right about books never changing – but people sure do. Case in point – moi! <u>Wuthering Heights</u> used to be my all-time favorite novel. The other day I needed a break from <u>Black Lamb</u> so I got myself a copy at Galignani – another notch on my bookstore list – and read it again. Geez Emily Brontë! Cathy didn't stand a co-dependent chance. Heathcliff was a total jerk. It made me realize books can also show us how we move on in life. Don't get me wrong – I'm glad I moved on from thinking all that damage was romantic – but it made me nostalgic too. Like I outgrew a childhood friend.

Au revoir and Have a Nice Day – I mean it,
Frida

P.S. I meant to write this up above – someone at the bookstore must take you seriously or you wouldn't have been hired.

1/2/92

Dear Frida,

Happy New Year! Thanks for the encouragement. I really appreciate it. It's just hard thinking about starting a new book. I spent over a year writing the last one, and then almost another year on revisions. But you're right. I'll never get published if I don't try again.

So what do I love enough to write a whole novel about it? That's a good question. I have a bunch of old notebooks in a box in my apartment, and I thought maybe if I looked through them I'd get some ideas. You should see all the notes I found about my Bumpa. When Franny and I were little, he was always telling us stories, and I guess at some point I started writing them down. Like how he went to Shanghai with the Navy in the 1930s. Can you imagine? An eighteen-year-old farm boy all of a sudden walking around China? And he raised my mom. I found a page about how my grandma told me when they got divorced she let him have custody. That kind of thing was unheard of in 1949, but she said she thought losing my mom might kill him, it would break his heart so much.

I really love Bumpa. It seems like he could be an interesting main character. Like someone in a Wallace Stegner novel (I just finished The Big Rock Candy Mountain). What do you think? I'm not sure because something weird has been happening. Yesterday I sat down to try writing about him, and all of a sudden my throat clenched and my stomach felt like a beehive. It was the same feeling I got the other day at work when Roy asked me how my writing is going. I even felt buzzing behind my eyelids. I had to hide in the coat closet and press my face against the cold wall until I could breathe again. I don't know what's happening to me.

Enough about my problems. At least one of our lives is on track. Those foreign correspondents are going to be so impressed by you. I'm on the hunt for more War Journo Dames. Until then I finally chose your next Surprise Me book. Every bookseller is assigned sections to take care of, and perky people get self-help, family, and cooking because none of the Serious Booksellers want them. A few weeks ago a customer asked for Serve It Forth by MFK Fisher. It was our last copy so I had to reorder. When it came in, I devoured it in one sitting. I didn't know people wrote about food like that or even that people write about food at all. You seem to really like food. I think you'll be into MFK as much as I am. I'm totally infatuated with the essay called "Borderland" where she describes how she heated tangerines on a radiator. Once you read it let me know if you have a secret food. (By the

way, for January I'm trying to hand-sell a hundred copies of <u>Serve It Forth</u>.)
Sincerely,
Kate

P.S. Nice try, but the reason I got hired at the bookstore was because they needed people to wrap books during Christmas, and I worked at a gift-wrapping store in a mall when I was in high school. You should see how nicely I can tie a bow.

FRIDA RODRIGUEZ ... EN ROUTE

January 15, 1992
Paris, France

Fair Kate,

How is it possible you don't know you're having anxiety attacks? There must be tons of books about them in your perky self-help section and haven't you listened to Nirvana? Your hot hometown band is one massive plaid-flannel-clad nervous breakdown. I'd also like to point out that the free coffee at work probably isn't helping the internal beehive.

I think you're on the right track with your idea about Bumpa. You can bet being a single dad wasn't <u>Three Men and a Baby</u> back in the day. It was probably strange for your mom too. I'm sorry it gives you anxiety but I hope you keep trying to write about it. Maybe my gift will help. Yesterday I was sitting in Chez Lisette and out in front the Seine is lined with bookstalls called bouquinistes – isn't that the most gorgeous word you've ever heard. It sounds like bouquets of books! I got up for a wander and found a stall that sells used American paperbacks. You'll never guess what I came across. Ha! Of course you will because you're holding it. I know you can get old Stegner's <u>Angle of Repose</u> at your store but it seemed like a message from the universe to find it here. If it doesn't inspire you, you can use it to swat the bees away.

Now for the bummer part of this letter. Thanks for MFK but no offense I'll pass. My mom has been writing about food for the <u>L.A. Times</u> since before I was born. I'd never say it to her but I don't get it. Who cares about the trend for Pacific Rim cookery when she got a master's degree in journalism from UCLA – that was back in the 1950s before women were getting master's in anything. Sure I love food. Kirby and I found a fromagerie nearby called Barthélémy that sells more than fifty – count 'em fifty! – kinds of goat cheese. We're going to try them all. A few at a time to save room since a couple doors down we discovered exquisite rabbit braised in mustard – but that's just good food. Everybody eats. Not everybody lives in a country at war. The destruction of innocent people's homes. The cruelty of bombs dropping on children. That's what's important.

Bonne journée – aka Have a Nice Day,

Frida

P.S. My secret food? No-brainer. Anything processed! When I was a kid I never got a single bowl of that psychedelic-orange Kraft mac and cheese. I used to sneak off to the Hostess thrift-shop and buy old Ding Dongs and eat them in my closet while my parents watched Masterpiece Theatre.

P.S. Deux. The bookstore kept you on after Christmas so you must have more going for you than knowing how to wrap a book.

1/28/92

Dear Frida,

Thank you so much for the Wallace Stegner. I know the words are the same in a copy I could get here, but it's better somehow coming from Paris and you. Double thanks for telling me about anxiety attacks. I tried cutting back to two cups of coffee a night, but they're getting worse. They've turned into this ~~totally nonstop~~ insistent stinging under my skin, and there's this claustrophobia, like I'm too close to myself. But there's a sort of distance at the same time, like I'm too far away. The other night I told Roy about it and he laughed so hard I thought he was going to pass out. He said of course I've never heard of anxiety attacks. I'm a bottled-up Scandinavian from the Pacific Northwest. He's from here, too, but he's African-American. I asked if that's why he's heard of them. That made him laugh harder. He said no, it's because he went to college in New York and everyone there is in therapy. I like Roy a lot. He's my age, and he's already lived in Paris. He was reading Gertrude Stein when he was in junior high, but he never makes me feel stupid, not even the time I mispronounced Anna Karenina.

KIM FAY

I guess Sven overheard our conversation about anxiety. The next time we were at the front counter together, he told me I should read Soren Kierkegaard (another name I had to look up). Sven says all anxiety is about choice, freedom, and ambiguous feelings. Then he went and bought me a copy of <u>Fear and Trembling</u>. I'm terrified he's going to ask me what I think about it. When I got back to my apartment, I opened it up, but the second I saw the word panegyric, the bees buzzed like crazy and I shoved it under my love seat.

Sometimes I worry I'll never understand writers like that. I mean, my mind's never worked that way before. I'm still wrapping it around MFK. It is definitely a bummer you don't want to read her. Not just because I like her (I can't help it, I just do), but because I wanted to pick another book you connected with like I did. It's hard to explain, but I can tell MFK knew exactly what she was meant to write. <u>Serve It Forth</u> was published when she was only twenty-nine. That means she wrote it when she was even younger. Every line feels like it came naturally to her, even though there's no way she was born knowing about ancient Egyptian dining customs and purifying escargots.

Time for a quick break to check on my soup (beef, leek, and barley).

I'm back. I'm trying a recipe from Laurie Colwin's <u>Home Cooking</u>, which is a cross between a memoir and a cookbook. She's kind of like MFK only friendlier. I like her because whenever she's writing about timbales or leeks or other food I've never heard of, she mixes it all in with her ideas about family and friendship and love. Things that don't seem like they have anything to do with food except she makes me think maybe they do. Laurie's sure of herself, too. She has no doubt that people want to read her thoughts on soup.

Did you know leeks are giant green onions? I bet you did. Like you know what a Jerusalem artichoke is. I had to look that up in <u>Larousse Gastronomique</u>. If you think <u>Black Lamb</u> is a biggie, it's a pip-squeak compared to <u>Larousse</u>. For the record, processed food is <u>not</u> my secret food. I'm a Kraft mac and cheese expert, and I ate my fair share of Pillsbury crescent rolls and Chef Boyardee pizza in a box when I was a kid. Not that I'm criticizing my mom or anything. Her pork chops are great, but she's more into things like water-skiing and horses. She even has trophies for barrel racing. She's just not a fan of cooking. I think it's because Bumpa was a bachelor. They ate lots of TV dinners when she was growing up.

Just looked at the clock. Lucky you. I have to run. I need to get to the bank before it closes to deposit my paycheck.
Have a Nice Day,
Kate

P.S. I did it again. I forgot to tell you about the book I'm sending. There's this ~~awesome~~ excellent used bookshop called Bowie & Company next door to my store. I was hunting around in their basement during my dinner break and found <u>Witness to War</u>. It's a biography of Marguerite Higgins. Have you heard of her? She's another War Journo Dame. I hope she makes up for MFK.

Frida Rodriguez … En Route

Bonjour Fair Kate,

Greetings from the Land of Learn Something New Every Day! Barrel racing? Qu'est-ce que c'est? I'm sitting here at Chez Lisette with Kirby, and he just filled me in. He says rodeos are a big thing in Washington. Your mom sounds cool. I can't imagine my mom racing a horse around barrels or water-skiing! When she was twenty-nine going on spinster – her words not mine – she married Dad who was forty-seven AND a widower AND had two daughters in their early twenties! If that wasn't scandalous enough in the antiquated 1960s, Mom's Scandinavian – the Danish variety – but not bottled-up – and Dad's family hailed from Mexico a couple generations ago.

Nothing like a youngish white mom and oldish Mexican dad to make gangly brace-face Frida stand out like a sore thumb. Plus Mom did these crackpot things like when my junior high had its annual culture night and parents were supposed to bring food – she brought sushi and wore a kimono. Same song second verse the year she brought samosas – she wore a sari! I told her she was supposed to bring something from OUR culture like aebleskivers or chiles rellenos but she said where's the education in that? She already knew about those foods. Then there are my half-sisters from Dad's first marriage – can you say overachievers? Dolores is a pediatric surgeon and Carmen is a public defender. People always think they're my aunts.

Geez I hope I'm not making it sound like we don't get along. Mom and Dad are still in love-love which is nice except sometimes when they kiss in public. People freak out a little even in this day and age when they've seen Jimmy Smits make out with a white woman on <u>L.A. Law</u> – unless they're in our neighborhood where we've lived all my life so people know us. He worships her and she's so nice she goes with him to the cemetery every year to put flowers on his first wife's grave. But imagine what it's like when you have friends over and your dad's playing Schubert on his violin while your mom dances in the middle of the living room wearing one of her floaty Isadora Duncan getups. Then when it's time for a snack she serves deviled eggs with capers and little blobs of caviar. Delish but just once I would have liked pigs in a blanket.

Speaking of therapy! It's like our letters are some kind of analyst's couch sucking me in. I was just telling Kirby how we barely know each other but for some reason I want to tell you everything about me. Don't worry. I won't. At least not now. I'm signing off. We have places to be. Kirby's a hybrid like me except not like me since he blends in with his green eyes and Kevin Bacon circa <u>Footloose</u> hair. His mom was born in Vietnam and he read about this grocery store called Thanh Binh in Place Maubert and wants to check it out. There are a few Vietnamese spots around the city but good luck finding a Mexican place. The other day I would have given up exclamation marks for a real taco! Alas I had to be satisfied with a bowl of chile con carne at Birdland.

You almost – but not quite – convinced me to read MFK. Ha! Have a Nice Day,
Frida

2/22/92

Dear Frida,

Did you ever get that snow you wanted? We just got a major surprise for this late in February. The whole city is snowed in. It started late this afternoon with these big feathery flakes like angels pillow fighting in the sky, and the store closed early before the buses stopped running. I read somewhere the city only has a couple snowplows. It's a real mess when we get a storm like this.

Highway 99 was already shut down so my bus went up First Avenue. The air was all crisp edges, and my favorite neon signs like Metsker Maps and Warshal's Sporting Goods looked like stained glass. Up at Pike Place the cobblestones were dusted with snow, and they shimmered crimson in the glow from the Public Market sign. The newsstand was the only place still open, with a few people inside bundled up in the amber light like a scene on a Christmas card. Along with working at a bookstore, I wanted to live in a big city when I was growing up, and tonight Seattle looked as magical as I imagined it would.

By the time the bus got to my stop in Ballard (the city's Scandinavian neighborhood with lots of old brick buildings like

Pioneer Square), everything was icy white. My apartment's on the second floor. Because I'm at the end of the building I have two brick walls. It's basically a long room with a ceiling sort of high enough for a kind of bedroom loft over the kitchen. I moved in last year, and every time I walk in I still think: A Room of My Very Own! I wonder what I'd think if I didn't learn about Virginia Woolf in college.

As soon as I got inside the power conked out. No buzzing fridge. No cars whooshing in the street. ~~It felt like being in a frozen cloud of It felt like having chilled cotton~~ I hate it when I can't find the right words. That's why I cross things out. It seems like some writers have the perfect word for every single thing, but I have to spend all this time searching my thesaurus because there are so many ways to use words that I never read when I was growing up, and I end up using the same ones, like awesome and totally. What am I, a Valley Girl?

I'm drinking a cup of Twinings blackcurrant tea, snuggled up on my love seat. Between my oil lamp and the moon off the snow, there's more than enough light to write to you. I think the snow is making me ~~thoughtful~~ introspective. I've been thinking about how different your childhood was from mine. I'm sorry it was embarrassing for you sometimes. It sounds ~~awesome~~ (there it is again) fascinating to me. You know about so many things I'm learning about for the first time reading your letters. Like capers and Isadora Duncan. And I can't imagine what it must be like to grow up in one place where everyone knows you.

My dad's a civil engineer, and he kept getting jobs all over the state. I think that's why I wrote what I did about being able to count on books. One time I ended up living in three places in a single year, but Sheila the Great and Harriet the Spy were up to the same old thing no matter where I was. Kind of like my family. It didn't matter where we lived. Dad would come into our bedroom at night and tell us one of his silly Raggedy Kojak mysteries that he started making up after our Raggedy Ann doll lost her hair. Mom would always find the local library and craft store for us, and Franny and I could play travel agent or <u>Charlie's Angels</u> wherever we were. We're pretty lucky. One thing I learned from all that moving is there are a lot of families out there that don't get along. We actually like each other. I mean, we can have fun doing pretty much anything together. Even if we're just driving to a store, we're talking a mile a minute or singing "Bad Moon Rising" at the top of our lungs. I get to see Mom and Dad a lot because they're only an hour away down in Olympia, but I really miss Franny. She graduated from college in California and got a job with a hotel down there. Our budgets don't have wiggle room for too many long-distance calls even now with the new evening rates.

Since I can only guess what therapy is like, to me our letters feel like writing in my diary but more satisfying because I know you're going to write back something that makes me think. It definitely isn't like my pen pal in the seventh grade. She lived in Wisconsin. All we wrote about were our favorite Lip Smacker flavors (Lipton lemonade for me) and our chances of marrying Shaun Cassidy.

I'm starting to doze off. Have a nice night,
Kate

P.S. I had to wait to mail this because of the snow. I ended up reading two books in the meantime, and now I have to tell you about them because I'm sending them to you. <u>The Debut</u> by Anita Brookner and <u>Eugénie Grandet</u> by Honoré de Balzac. The reason I read <u>Eugénie</u> is because Anita writes about it in <u>The Debut</u>. Her main character, Ruth, thinks her life has been ruined by literature because she read the wrong kinds of books growing up. Fairy tales where the wicked get punished and the good live happily ever after. But Ruth was good, and she didn't get a happy ending. Ruth thinks if she read more realistic books like <u>Eugénie</u> she would've been better prepared for life. Do you think that's true? When I try to think about it, the bees go into overdrive.

P.P.S. I hope it's not corny to send you a picture of me, but I'm curious about what you look like, so maybe you feel the same way.

FRIDA RODRIGUEZ … EN ROUTE

March 7, 1992
Paris, France

Bonjour Pen Pal,

My fave Lip Smacker was Dr Pepper and I was going to marry Scott Baio and STOP talking about what you don't know. I never heard of a barrel racer until I met you. And by the way sometimes things are TOTALLY AWESOME!

Yes – I was curious. You look like I imagined and kind of like Alice in Wonderland too with that headband. Kirby took the pic I'm sending at the Christmas market outside Notre-Dame. That's red wine down the side of my stirrup pants not blood – I should never wear light colors and vin chaud should never be served to go!

When I was reading about your family I got this vision in my head. It's like you guys were on a boat that traveled from port to port. The ports were different but the boat was always the same. Now you don't live on the boat anymore but you have sea legs so you feel wobbly on land. Think about it. Maybe the wobbliness is your anxiety. I know what I'm trying to say but I'm not sure it's coming out right. The only self-help book I've read was Mom's copy of <u>The Woman's Dress for Success Book</u>, and I don't think advice to carry an attaché case and only wear colorless nail polish is relevant.

Have you noticed you use a lot of details when you describe locations? I wonder if it's because you moved around so much – it made you aware of your surroundings more – not like people who stay in one place and get used to what's around them. I can see the bookstore. I can see Seattle in the snow. Angels having a pillow fight – totally awesomely vivid! I'm good at who what when and why but I could use more practice on the where. Ready for it?

I picked La Louisiane because it's in my budget in the Saint-Germain-des-Prés quarter where intellectuals hung out back in the day. The building looks super Parisian. Typewriter screeches to a halt. Super Parisian? Seriously Frida! Would Martha write anything as gauche as that?

Be kind, rewind . . .

The hotel is more than a hundred years old. It's six floors with a façade the color of bygone times. Does bygone times sound like I'm trying too hard? I know what you mean about searching for the perfect words. Sometimes a word is technically right but it doesn't capture the true feeling of something. Like when I look at this building I feel history shaking loose and doing a cool jazz scat down in the streets. How do I find a word that captures that?

I thought I was moving into any old budget hotel but no! Jean-Paul Sartre lived here. Tell that to Old Sven. Simone de Beauvoir lived here. Juliette Gréco had her star-crossed love affair with Miles Davis here. He was in Paris doing the soundtrack for a movie called <u>Ascenseur pour l'échafaud</u> – I've practically worn out the cassette on my Walkman already. I heard that he wanted to be with her forever but it was the 1950s and he said he wouldn't take her back to the U.S. because he loved her too much to make her unhappy being married to a black man there – and she was shocked because she said in Paris she didn't notice his color. Can that be true? I've had a few people comment on my skin but I don't know if it's like America where color is <u>everything</u>.

A lot of people live here at the hotel like it's an apartment building. They have paintings on their walls and shelves brimming with books. I inherited a hot plate from whoever had this room last – I don't use it much – why would I? – Chez Lisette is less than five minutes away for my morning oeufs cocotte and café au lait. Lisette has been giving me free food because I help her clean up at the end of the night. I'd do it without the freebies. She always seems tired when it's time to close up.

Did I tell you I read the Marguerite bio? She convinced the <u>New York Herald Tribune</u> to send her to cover WWII – when she was only twenty-four! – even younger than MFK when she wrote about purifying escargots. I don't have connections so I've been wondering if I should just go someplace like Czechoslovakia or Croatia and let the assignment find me like Martha did when she went to the Spanish war – at only twenty-nine!

I also gulped down <u>The Debut</u> and <u>Eugénie Grandet</u> and have a bone to pick with Anita and Balzac. Sure it's good to be prepared for this cold cruel world – but are they saying don't even try to be a good person since life might give you the short end of the stick no matter what you do? That sounds like a Gloomy Gertie way to live. No thanks!

Have a Nice Day!

Frida

From the desk of Kate Fair
who's at the Evergreen Mobile Home Park
so she's using this old yellow notepad for stationery

3/18/92

Dear Frida,

Thanks for sending a picture back. I imagined you with long messy-wavy hair like Julia Roberts in <u>Pretty Woman</u>, but you're Demi Moore in <u>Ghost</u>. I could never look that great in a pixie.

I'm jealous of your description of your hotel. You said you can see everything I describe, but I can feel everything you describe. Like "history shaking loose and doing a cool jazz scat down in the streets." I wish I knew how to do that. (And I don't mean to talk about things I don't know, but it's the truth that I had to look up Jean-Paul Sartre, Simone de Beauvoir, Juliette Gréco, AND Miles Davis.)

I'm at Bumpa's place for a few days. He lives in Bothell about half an hour east from me across Lake Washington. I had to borrow a car, which is part of the reason I'm here. He works these car auctions, and he thinks I can get something decent for a couple hundred bucks. I didn't used to mind the bus. It can get stinky, but funny things happen sometimes. Like when I found a bus pass, and I tracked down the old woman to return it. She gave me a pair of L'eggs pantyhose to thank me. How random is that? But last week a lady sat down beside me and saw me reading <u>Anna Karenina</u>. I've been reading it for over two months. The woman opened her big mouth and said, "My heart dropped into my stomach when Anna . . ." I won't say it in case you haven't read it. She ~~totally~~ ruined it for me. I can take the bad smells, but I can't risk someone spoiling another book like that.

I also need a car so I can come over here more often and write down Bumpa's stories. I'm interviewing him now, and I'm trying to look at his world like a writer would, since he's going to be my main character. I'm not sure what details I'll use yet, but I want to be able to describe whatever I do use perfectly. Even if it's just the drive into his mobile home park. The park is surrounded by towering evergreens, and I know it's big, but it reminds me of <u>The Secret Garden</u>, the way it feels hidden from the outside world. All the trailers have miniature front yards, and people care a lot about their flowers. This is the prettiest time of year to be here because the rhodies are starting to bloom.

Really examining this place got me thinking about your boat theory. Just like the boat was always the same, there were some harbors like here where everything stayed the same, too. I mean, when I drove under the canopy beside Bumpa's trailer yesterday, he was already waiting on the porch beside the lilac bush. How does he do that? How does he know I'm about to pull up? There are lots of bigger trailers here, but his is a single-wide. It's snug, and I think he likes it because it's long and narrow like all the different ships he worked on. Here's another thing that never changes. As soon as I got out of the car, the first thing he said was, "Hey Punkin, that's a snazzy green velvet fedora you're wearing." I pretended to tip a hat and replied, "Why thank you. I really like your pink polka-dot waistcoat." I have no idea when we started that, but we do it every time we see each other. It's even funnier because I'm definitely not a crazy dresser, and he almost always wears brown slacks and one of his brown plaid shirts with a white t-shirt underneath. He even still uses the same Timex we gave him for Christmas when I was little.

His trailer is pretty much no-frills, too. That makes the things he does have stand out. Like the candy dish on the coffee table. It's one of those old-fashioned kinds made out of green glass, and he keeps black licorice in it because Franny and I <u>love</u> black licorice. He only ever had an old painting of a schooner on the living room wall until I graduated from college and then Franny last year. Our graduation pictures are hanging over the couch now. He left school after the eighth grade, and he used to say the only thing he wanted in life was for us to get college degrees.

It's interesting analyzing what parts of him might belong in a novel and how I'd do it. He made our usual canned tamales for dinner, and when we played gin rummy afterward, he told me one of his stories about when he was first mate on the Brown Bear. That was a University of Washington research vessel up in Alaska. He worked on it a few summers when Mom was in junior high, and he says she was so horse crazy, she'd stay at his brother Ralph's ranch to ride horses all summer long. This seemed like a perfect opportunity, so I asked Bumpa what it felt like being a single dad in the 1950s. It's hard to explain the look he got on his face. It was kind of confused, and he said, "I never thought about it, Punkin." I waited for him to say more, but he kept playing cards and went back to talking about the Brown Bear.

Later on in bed, I started wondering if it was weird that Bumpa never thought about it. What do you think? Is his not thinking about it relevant to my story? Not that I know what my story is. I tried to imagine what trendy authors like Susan Minot or Barbara Kingsolver would consider important. I mean, if I'm going to write this novel, I need to get everything just right.

You know how it is after midnight when your mind can't rest? Time felt kind of furry. Plus the buzzing started up. Quietly, but I can sense when the bees are coming now. I was pretty sure I wouldn't be getting back to sleep anytime soon. The book I've been reading (If You Want to Write) was in the living room, and when I got up to get it, Bumpa was bent over the dining table with a bunch of radio parts spread out on a newspaper. All the lights were off except one lamp so he could see what he was doing. He's always buying old broken electronics at garage sales so he can tinker with them. He looked up and said, "Your mom used to wake up in the middle of the night, too. She's a night owl like me." I got myself a cup of coffee. It had that burnt taste because he'll keep turning the coffee maker on and off so he can drink the whole pot before starting another, even if it takes a couple days.

I wanted to try asking him about raising Mom again. Maybe I didn't ask the right way before. But I wanted to just sit there with him, too, and watch him hunt through trays of vacuum tubes and resistors for the right parts. I don't know why, but I've always loved looking at his hands while he works on one of his projects. Even though his jobs were on ships all his life, his hands aren't rough, and he has long, elegant fingers with nails that are perfectly curved like polished shells.

He asked if I wanted to help, and he reminded me how to use the little machine to test the tubes. It's easy to putter in silence with Bumpa, and we worked together for a while until the bees settled down. I was getting a little hungry, and I didn't feel like having any licorice, so I made us some scrambled eggs. When I handed Bumpa his plate, he smiled at it and said, "It sure is nice to be awake with someone else when the rest of the world is asleep." I could picture him and Mom in the middle of the night when she was growing up, probably playing canasta, and I wondered if she felt the same way I did. Outside in the velvety darkness, the pine trees whispered in the breeze, and the lamp made this kind of golden cocoon around us, like Bumpa and I were the only two people in the world. Maybe it's not the kind of interesting thing people want to read about in a book, but he's right, Frida. It is nice.

Love,

Kate

March 29, 1992
Paris, France

Bonjour Kate,

Remember how I told you Kirby met some foreign correspondents he was going to introduce me to? Well one of them is back in Paris and Kirby brought him to Chez Lisette the other night. Niko is the bureau chief for <u>Current</u> covering the breakup of Yugoslavia – he's here for a week and I asked him if I could pick his brain and . . . !!!

!!!We've been out three nights in a row!!! I swear he knows every restaurateur in this city. No matter where we go as soon as he walks in the door they shout, "Ah, Niko, ça va?" We had oysters on the half shell at Goumard-Prunier – the first restaurant in Paris to serve raw oysters like that all the way back in the 1800s – brilliant! – and scallops in apple cider sauce at Pharamond. Mom can do some amazing things with scallops, but that cider stirred with cream – my taste buds are still trembling! I'm not materialistic but Fair Kate it's a plain fact that it's nicer to eat out with a man who has an expense account.

After food and wine and more wine we bundled up in coats and scarves and walked along the Seine. He told me about the wars and revolutions he's covered. Romania, El Salvador, Lebanon. Last night he wrapped me in his arms and I could see Notre-Dame lit up behind him and he whispered into my ear about how he'll never run out of work because the world will never run out of wars. When I told him about reading Martha and Marguerite he kissed my eyelids and when I quoted from <u>Moon Tiger</u> about this being a century of wars he said we were destined to meet.

Thank you my fair bookselling pen pal for bringing these marvelous women into my life so I could impress tall dark handsome Niko Andrianakis on the banks of the Seine. He's not worldly just because he's thirty-four. His parents are diplomats and he grew up in Hong Kong, Buenos Aires, and Madrid. He speaks six – count 'em SIX – languages. He dated an actress from <u>Falcon Crest</u>! I can't believe he's leaving for Sarajevo tomorrow. Bosnia declared its independence and he says it could get bad there like in Croatia because the Bosnian Serbs are going to fight it. They want to stay part of Yugoslavia. He promised he'll write and the next time he's in Paris we'll see each other again. I can imagine us working together. This could turn out to be the beginning of my career and maybe even my whole life.

Now let's talk about <u>your</u> career. You're worrying too much right now about what's important and what's not. Finish interviewing Bumpa – figure out your plot – then see what fits and what doesn't. I have a gut feeling you'll find a perfect spot for Bumpa and your mom playing cards in the middle of the night <u>and</u> you'll make it interesting. And for the record it's definitely not weird that Bumpa didn't think about being a single dad. Guys from his generation didn't have sensitive Phil Donahue types to teach them how to think about stuff like that but that doesn't mean you can't use your very own clever imagination to describe what it was like. That's what writers do and you're a writer Fair Kate!

Have a Nice Day!

Frida

P.S. Niko thinks my typewriter is adorable but he says journalism is about technology now. The Soviet Union wouldn't have collapsed without the fax and since the Gulf War all the TV news outlets want are live satellite broadcasts. Except when you're in the field he says the Reporter's Note Book is still your best friend. He gets his from a place called Stationers in Virginia – he's like having my very own graduate program! – and those soft kisses! – I miss him already!!

P.S. Deux. I got my hair cut right before I moved here. I copied the style from Jean Seberg in À bout de souffle. It's my favorite French New Wave movie.

P.S. Trois. What's a canned tamale?

From the desk of Kate Fair
who's at the Evergreen Mobile Home Park <u>again</u>
so she's <u>still</u> using this old yellow notepad for stationery

4/14/92

Dear Frida,

Oh! My! Gosh! We both have kisses to tell!! You're never going to believe this.

OLD SVEN!! (He's actually not that old. Only two years older than me.)

Did I mention he hosts our reading series? The night Lydia Minatoya was here for her memoir, the stars aligned. After the reading he heard me mention how I borrowed a car again. His Dart was in the shop and he asked for a ride home since Wallingford is almost on the way to Ballard. When we got to his house we started talking. I know it's not a walk on the Seine, but it had rained all day, and I can't imagine any place more radiant than Seattle after a downpour. Through the windshield we could see all the way down to Lake Union where the skyline looked like sequins reflecting off the water.

I can't believe everything we told each other. I confessed how terrified I am of Kierkegaard. I told him more about my anxiety and how it especially happens when I'm writing, and he said it's the sign of being a truly creative person. I even told him how I wanted to be Pinky Tuscadero when I was in the third grade before I decided to write books. He wanted to be an Air Force pilot but he got diabetes when he was sixteen. It was hard for him to accept, but he thinks his disappointment will make him a better novelist. Yes, he wants to be a novelist, too! The next thing I knew he leaned over the gearshift and kissed me. Right then the radio played R.E.M.'s "Shiny Happy People." Can you believe it?

We haven't told a single soul. Yesterday on our dinner break I left first. He left a few minutes later. We met up at Bud's Jazz Records around the corner. There's a narrow stairwell that goes down from the sidewalk to the shop underground, and we felt like spies rendezvousing on a secret mission. We got so lost in the liner notes on your Miles Davis soundtrack we were late getting back to the store. We had to make up an excuse about how we ran into each other at the Merchants Cafe, and they messed up our orders so we had to wait. The last thing we need is a bunch of gossipy opinions about Serious Sven and Perky Kate.

Sven says he loves knowing the me no one else at the store knows. When I get to work, he asks me how my ladies are doing. He means Anita Brookner and Margaret Drabble (she's another British novelist I'm into right now). It's our inside joke. We sneak into the coat closet and kiss. And I help him dodge the Middle-Aged Lady Poets who are madly in love with him. You would not believe how many Middle-Aged Lady Poets there are in Seattle who madly love Sven.

Frida, it's like my life changed in an instant. Every night after work Sven comes over to my place, and we drink tea and read out loud to each other. I just thought of a perfect word without having to look in my Roget's. Now that I'm with Sven every second feels luminous. And not just when I'm with him. Like right now, being here at Bumpa's. It's one of my favorite places in the entire world, but tonight I'm really seeing how special it is for me. I think I forgot to tell you how when Dad traveled for work and Mom went with him, they'd drop Franny and me off here. We'd eat black licorice for dinner and play pool for hours at the clubhouse across the street, and Bumpa had this funny little Peugeot moped he let us drive all by ourselves as long as we didn't leave the park. It felt like being at the center of the universe.

Last night while Bumpa and I were playing gin, I kept thinking how lucky I am to have such ~~an awesome~~ a loving grandpa. Do you know my mom says she's never heard him say an unkind word about anyone. And my whole loving family – my Love Boat. Ha! And Sven. I have Sven. I can't stop smiling. I feel giddy. Is that how Niko makes you feel? He sounds amazing. Diplomat parents and bureau chief for Current magazine. My dad's had a subscription for as long as I can remember, and now that I'm at the store he clips out book reviews that sound interesting and mails them to me. I'm sorry Niko left for Sarajevo. I hope you get to see him again soon.

Until then here are some more books to help you on your War Journo Dame journey. The last time I was at Bowie & Company poking around, I couldn't believe your luck. I found nearly perfect copies of Marguerite Higgins' News Is a Singular Thing AND

<u>War in Korea</u> AND <u>Our Vietnam Nightmare</u>. I guess they were all together because they came from an estate sale. I want you to have them as a thank-you gift. Can you believe we've been writing to each other for half a year? We've never met, but I feel like whatever I tell you, you'll understand it, like we're on the same wavelength or something. It's not always like that with my old friends anymore. A lot of them are already getting married, and they talk about things like having babies and mortgage plans. I'm into Sven, but I can't imagine that right now.

Have a divine day!

Kate

P.S. I've never seen a French New Wave movie, but I think I like foreign films. I can't wait to see <u>Enchanted April</u>.

P.P.S. Hormel tamales come in a can with this tangy red sauce. You heat them up, peel off the wrappers, and fold them in bread with a ton of margarine. It has to be Wonder bread so you can squish it really good. My mouth is watering just thinking about it.

P.P.P.S. I've been wearing the Eiffel Tower scrunchie every day. Thank you. I love it. Where did you find it?

FRIDA RODRIGUEZ ... EN ROUTE

April 27, 1992
Paris, France

Fair Kate,

Were you in a rush when you sent me those Marguerite books? Did you see all the treasures inside? Jackpot city! A 1973 receipt from the Raffles Hotel in Singapore, a 1968 newspaper clipping about Jimi Hendrix, a 1986 TWA ticket to Lisbon, a Disneyland E ticket, a receipt from Chubby & Tubby for a doghouse, a prescription for something called Miltown, three dry-cleaning tickets, two grocery lists — and a partridge in a pear tree – ha! I love finding things in used books. I try to imagine the person who owned them before me. I have all this stuff spread out on the bed, and whoever owned these is a real head-scratcher.

Thanks to you too. When I wrote to the store asking for Martha it felt good to have someone interested in the kind of life I'm trying to live now. I get what you're saying about old friends. Mine write me letters about why men shouldn't wear parachute pants or how they want to have kids and name the girls Brittany and the boys Zach. It can make me sad like what I said about <u>Wuthering Heights</u> and the way we move on in life.

Not to get all mushy or anything but I can tell how whenever you pick out a book for me you care about how I'm trying to learn as much as I can so I'll be prepared when I figure out where I should go. I'm starting to think it really is Bosnia. Are you getting news about it over there? Snipers opened fire on peace demonstrators and Serb forces started shelling Sarajevo and now the city is under siege. You learn about that kind of stuff in history class – the Siege of Leningrad – but they teach it like it's all in the past. This is 1992!

I haven't heard from Niko. Not like he can jot postcards while he's at war – hey babe wish you were here – but I wish there was a better way of knowing he's okay than scouring the pages of Current. Meeting him has made me realize how lame I've been just reading my War Journo Dames and waiting for it to be Frida's turn. I went to the Yugoslavian embassy to find out what I need to do to get a visa. The answer – a publication has to write a letter saying I work for them so I can get press credentials. I wrote to one of my professors from college and asked for her help. I'm waiting to hear back – I feel like all I've been doing is waiting – drifting along eating goat cheese and why have I been so passive? Frida Rodriguez is not passive!

Last but not least – hold the phone! – Old Sven!? Who has a name like that anymore? Does he look like a Viking? Can you believe I met my journalist and you met your novelist at the same time? The world works in mysterious ways. Tell me more about being giddy and smiling all the time. Take my mind off all this waiting!

Your impatient friend,
Frida

P.S. I found an Eiffel Tower scarf at a tourist stall, and I was going to send it as is when a round of Metro roulette landed me at a whole neighborhood of fabric shops around Sacré-Coeur. That's when I got the idea to buy elastic and a sewing kit and make it into a scrunchie. I'm glad you like it. I was worried you might only wear headbands.

P.S. Deux. I think canned tamales are the one place I'll skip processed food. Mom may be from Danish stock, but if God ever threw a fiesta, her tamales would top the menu. Food these days is all unsaturated this and lo-fat that, but she still uses lard. That's the delicious trick.

5/12/92

Dear Frida,

I hope you've heard from Niko by now. I've been reading his
articles in <u>Current</u>. Confession: I don't understand the difference
between Bosnians, Bosnian Serbians, Serbians, and Serbian nationalists. It's hard to get a handle on this war. It's not like when
we invaded Iraq. It was pretty black and white, and that's all anyone was talking about at the store. Even though Sarajevo is on
NPR, people don't seem to get riled up in the same way. I asked
Sven if maybe it's because it's so confusing to figure out who's
who, but he says it's because the average person doesn't care if it
isn't on the cover of <u>People</u> or doesn't involve them. That second
part especially seems true since when I heard about the riots in
L.A., my first thought was your family and if they're safe. That
made it feel more real to me. I mean it's horrific no matter what,
but knowing you made me pay attention even more.

I've been thinking about how you and I can't imagine having
families anytime soon. Mom and Dad were high school sweet-
hearts and got married right after she graduated. They're still in

love-love like your parents, and people talk about what a great couple they are. You'd think I would have been desperate for my college boyfriend to propose so I could have that, too. He was a nice guy, and he'll for sure make a great dad. But I felt restless when I was with him. I've never told anyone that before.

As for Sven looking like a Viking, this is going to sound ~~totally~~ sappy, but there's an essence of the era of fountain pens about him. He has blond curls that make me think of the pictures of Keats and Shelley hanging in the poetry section, minus the pale porcelain skin. If there's anything Nordic about him, it's how healthy he looks. When you combine that with his ~~massive~~ tenacious intelligence, I think it makes it hard for people to understand how sick he is. We start talking when we get home from work and don't stop until dawn and sometimes not even until we have to go back to the store in the afternoon. I fell asleep at the info desk twice this week. When we're deep in a conversation, I look down and see our fists clenched. I think it's because we're holding on so tightly to each other's words.

He's not like me. He knows exactly what he wants to write, and you're never going to believe it. His novel is about how even if you're a good person, life will still disappoint you, and the constant struggle to keep on being a good person once you realize this. That's the exact same thing Anita and Balzac write about. It's so interesting to talk to him about everything I'm reading. The other night, I read him the MFK essay, about secret eating where she puts tangerines on the radiator, and he doesn't think it's about secret foods at all. He thinks she's writing about how people construct happiness. It's just a tangerine, but MFK gave meaning to the hot crackle of the shell and the cold rush of pulp so it would bring her pleasure. Sven says this is what people do to protect themselves from life's constant disappointments. Like how I tend my windowsill garden or read breezy writers like Laurie Colwin. Or my nightly tea ritual. He loves that. I guess maybe it's true. When I'm down, thinking about how my novel didn't get published and things like that, it does make me feel better to steep tea in the little white pot Mom gave me when I moved into this apartment. I just didn't realize it was a ritual or that I was constructing happiness until we talked about it.

Love,

Kate

P.S. I found a <u>Three's Company</u> trading card in the copy of Anne Tyler's <u>A Slipping-Down Life</u> I bought next door. How ~~strange~~ incongruous is that? I love finding weird things in used books, too.

FRIDA RODRIGUEZ ... EN ROUTE

May 28, 1992
Paris, France

Dear Kate,

The world is repugnant! I hate it! <u>HATE</u>! They're shelling
Red Cross convoys on their way into Sarajevo and yesterday there
was a mortar attack on a breadline outside a bakery – twenty-six
people died – trying to get something to eat! AND! The riots in
L.A.! I'm furious! I can't believe those disgusting cops weren't
convicted! Who am I kidding? Of course they weren't!

Want to know the stupid frosting on the stupid cake? I told
Kirby how I'm worried about Niko and still waiting to hear from
my professor and the whole world is going nutso while I'm sitting
in a hotel in Paris reading books about women who did something about it. I'm ready to BE one of those women doing something about it! Do you know what he had the nerve to say? He
asked me if I really think I'm ready. He made it sound like I don't
know what war's really like. Just because he studies buildings
destroyed in wars, he's an expert? Now we're mad at each other
and we've only gotten through twenty-eight goat cheeses at the
fromagerie. How else am I supposed to distract myself? Why did
he have to go and ruin a good thing?!?

AHHHHH!

Calgon take me away! Tell me MORE about Sven. Construct some happiness to divert my attention from how lousy life is!
Your grumpy pen pal who is NOT having a Nice Day,
Frida

P.S. Sorry – I should have led with this – I'm just so mad. My family is fine if anyone can be fine in a city world universe that is so not fine!

THE PUGET SOUND BOOK COMPANY

101 South Main Street   Seattle, WA 98104

6/16/92

Dear Frida,

I'm relieved to know your family is okay. And you're right. The world is repugnant. I don't have a TV so I got my news about the riots on NPR. When the National Guard was called in and the mayor declared a state of emergency, there was this one guy they interviewed who talked about how he lived in a nice neighborhood and the riots were wrecking his property value. How disgusting is that. People were actually losing their homes. They were dying. That's what he should have been upset about.

It feels weird that there are so many good things to tell you with everything that's happening in places like Sarajevo and L.A. Like the night Sven snuck outside to pick lilacs from the bush across the street so when I woke up there were clouds of purple all over the apartment. We already have "our restaurant." Lombardi's up the street. Have you ever had roasted garlic? It's creamy, stinky heaven on a slice of bread. We saw the Tiny Hat Orchestra at the Backstage after dinner one night, but best of all was when Sven took me on a picnic a few weeks ago. I'm thinking we'll go to a park, sit on a blanket, and eat the liverwurst sandwiches I made with Brie and fresh-baked mini boules from Ballard Market. Brie's a new one for me, too. Butter-flavored cheese. How did I not know about it?

Anyhow, he parked near Pike Place Market so I figured we were going somewhere overlooking Elliott Bay and the Olympics. But he carried our basket in the opposite direction to the Frederick & Nelson department store. A while ago I told him how sad I am about it closing. Every Christmas Mom and Dad drove Franny and me into Seattle to look at The Bon star and get Santa pictures taken at Freddy's (that's what everyone calls it). Can you believe it was the same Santa every year?

It turns out it was the store's final day. The doorman opened the big brass doors for us, and when we walked inside, my heart crumbled. Everything was on massive sale, and I'm not comparing the situations or anything like that, but it kind of looked a little bit like some of the pictures of the looted places in L.A. in the newspaper. One woman was carrying so many furs she could barely walk. I looked around at all that elegant mahogany and marble, and I could feel the building mourning.

Sven led the way downstairs to the Arcade, and it took everything in my power not to burst into tears. Where else can you find a camera shop, record shop, stationery shop, international newsstand, shoe repair, and gourmet food shop all in one place? Malls aren't the same. I was so preoccupied I didn't realize at first what Sven was doing. Right there in front of the delicacy shop, he spread a blanket on the floor. Then he took out a tiny bottle of champagne. When a salesgirl saw our plastic cups, she went to the café and gave us real champagne glasses.

We sat down right there and toasted to the end of an era. I told Sven that thinking about all the times I came here makes me sad because that part of my childhood can never happen again. He held my hand and said, "We'll make new childhoods for our own children. With your eyes and cheekbones, my lips, and a combination of our noses, they'll be beautiful." How corny is that? I'm such a sap. I loved it. I know what I said about not being ready for a family yet. That hasn't changed, but I felt so happy it scared me. When I asked Sven if I was scared because I was constructing happiness to keep disappointment at bay, he said no, this happiness was real, and that's what made it so scary.

Love,

Kate

P.S. I'm getting a reputation next door at Bowie & Company. The owner showed me a book he found at another estate sale. <u>Front Line</u> by Clare Hollingworth. He said he's been keeping an eye out for books by War Journo Dames for me. When I told him about you, he gave me a discount. It turns out Clare was only a week into her first job for <u>The Daily Telegraph</u> when she was driving around all by herself and saw Germans massing troops and tanks on the Polish border. She wrote about it and became the Very First Person to report the outbreak of WWII. She wasn't really ready for war either, but maybe that's not how these things work. Probably no one's ready until they're in one. If journalists let that stop them, no one would go. Don't be mad at Kirby. I bet he's worried about you. He doesn't want you to get hurt. He probably has a crush on you, too. Any guy would.

P.P.S. I asked our special orders department to track down some Reporter's Note Books for you. I hope a dozen is enough.

FRIDA RODRIGUEZ ... EN ROUTE

July 2, 1992
Paris, France

Dear Kate,

THANK YOU for the Reporter's Note Books! Best Present Ever!! And perfect timing. Niko's back in Paris and get this: Not only did my professor get me a letter from a paper called <u>Alt News L.A.</u> – Niko says there's no better way to become a War Journo than baptism by fire. Ready or not – now that the UN has control of the airport and I have my credentials letter, Niko's pretty sure he can get me into Sarajevo!

I shouldn't have told Kirby. He says Niko's being irresponsible. I reminded him of all the trial-by-fire War Journo Dames I've been reading. I told him what you said about how it's impossible to be ready until you've done it but I know the risks. Not that I'm going to carry a revolver like old Clare – thanks for her memoir – it gives me courage every time I read about another woman who did what I want to do. Anyway things got heated. Kirby said reading isn't doing, and I flew off the handle and did something stupid. I accused him of being jealous of Niko. Now he's not talking to me at all which is awkward in a hotel with only one tiny elevator.

That's a gloomy note to end on. How about this instead? Old Sven sounds perfect for you and what a romantic. That picnic – swoon – look out Lloyd Boom Box Dobler! I hope the candied lilacs make it to you without getting crushed. I figure you two lovebirds can nibble on them while you read to each other.

Lots to do before I leave. Have a Happy Day – the real kind not the constructed kind!

Frida

7/20/92

Dear Frida,

Another late night at the store. After my front counter shift, I finished doing inventory. Tonight I checked my cooking section. We need to reorder <u>The Silver Palate Cookbook</u> again, and somebody finally bought the ragged little booklet about cooking with roses. I won't reorder that one. According to my printout, it's been languishing on the shelf since 1987.

Now I'm at the information desk. Roy's sitting across from me. Have I described him to you yet? He has huge brown eyes and this booming laugh that doesn't match how slim he is. He's been reading Denise Levertov's poems out loud, and he has the most soothing voice. ~~It resonates through~~ I call him the Bee Whisperer. Denise lives here in Seattle, and whenever she comes in, Roy talks to her about her poetry like she's a regular person. I feel fuzzy when an author even smiles at me.

The travel section is in the alcove behind me, and poetry, essays, and fiction are in the sections behind Roy. All along the shelves, little index cards stick out, kind of like the Tibetan prayer flags hanging in the Eastern religion section. They're our staff recommendations. They make me think of messages in bottles, except instead of calls for help, they offer help to the person who needs that specific book right now. I think being able to recommend the right book at the right time is one of the most important things I can do with my life. I really hope I'll write a novel that will be the exact book a person needs at a certain time in their life.

I don't know why I wrote about the store tonight. Sometimes I just get this urge to describe a place. The other night during one of our midnight tea-and-talk marathons, I told Sven what you said about how maybe it's because I moved around so much, and that made me extra observant. He thinks it's a good theory but there might be more to it. Like I have a need to pin places down to help me feel safe. When I asked him safe from what, he said the vulnerability of my unpredictable childhood. I never thought about my childhood being unpredictable, but I guess maybe it was. Sven reads every author who does a reading at the store, and when he was talking to this one about her ideas the other night, she told him she's never felt so articulated. He really does have an ability to articulate things in ways I've never considered before.

I also think maybe I'm avoiding your news about Niko. Of course I'm excited that he wants to take you to Sarajevo, but I'm scared for you, too. Do you know when you're leaving?
Love,
Kate

7/26/92

Dear Frida,

I know I just wrote to you, but I have big news. Sven and I let the cat out of the bag today. You're not going to believe this. One of our co-workers, Josephine who shelves the kids books, started calling us the Golden Couple (not even facetiously, and she's really facetious like Dorothy Parker). Everyone seems happy for us. Except the Middle-Aged Lady Poets, of course. And Dawn (she's the one who scolded me for telling people to have a nice day). She wears caftans and has the New Age section, and when Sven told her I almost had my novel published, she said she wasn't surprised it failed because I won't have anything important to say until I'm forty.

I wasn't happy he told her what happened, but I guess it was an accident. She'd said something rude about how I'm not on his intellectual level, so he told her how Little, Brown wanted my novel. Then she asked why it's not in the store. That's when he realized he put his foot in it and had to explain the whole story. I don't get why she's so mad at me. She's married. I hate how she watches me out of the corner of her eye. Is it so impossible Sven likes me?

Confession: What if she's right? He thinks so much more than the average human being. I'm pretty much an average human being. When we went to a revival of <u>Annie Hall</u> at the Neptune, there's that scene where Alvy is talking about aesthetic criteria, and Annie thinks how she's not smart enough for him. What if I'm not smart enough for Sven? His mind is (attention, please, for the perfect word): lithe.

. . . I had to step away. A suspicious-looking guy slunk into the back room. We're on high alert because people are stealing <u>The Anarchist Cookbook</u> more than usual lately. Roy says maybe there's going to be an uprising if George Bush gets reelected.

Where was I? I just wish my anxiety would go away. Sometimes when Sven and I are talking, I start to disintegrate. I swear I'm made of gauze. I can literally feel the air on my bones. Like when I told him your theory about the boat. He thinks it's an excellent example of constructing happiness. He said I constructed a perfect life on the boat to keep me safe from the unpredictability, but since it's not keeping me safe out in the world, how real could it have been? Stupid bees. They buzzed like crazy when I wrote that.

I get why he doesn't understand my family. I can't believe I forgot to tell you I met his parents. Talk about the polar opposite from mine. They had us over for dinner, and it started out okay. They were asking me about myself, do I have any hobbies, brothers or sisters, the usual parent questions. For some reason I told them how I played tennis in high school and whenever I looked up beside the court, Mom and Dad were there. Sometimes Mom still had paint on her jeans because she'd been working on our house (she was always working on the house), and Dad was usually in a suit because he came from work. Sven's mom is a nurse. She smiled at me and said, "How nice. I moved to the swing shift once Sven got into school. I've never enjoyed being a mother."

Who says something like that? Right in front of him! Who does something like that? Sven needed her. Diabetes is no joke. He has to check his blood sugar three times a day, give himself shots, and eat at specific times so he won't pass out and die. The other night his blood sugar levels plummeted, and he started sweating and shaking. He practically shouted at me to get him a Snickers. I can't imagine what that must have felt like when it was new to him and he was home all alone. I wonder if he ever constructed any kind of happiness to keep himself safe from that.

Love,

Kate

FRIDA RODRIGUEZ ... EN ROUTE

August 15, 1992
Paris, France

Dear Kate,

Can you believe I'm leaving in a week!? My visa is for two weeks, but who knows if I'll end up staying longer. If I do I'll send an address but for now keep writing to the hotel. I'm racing to get supplies. Niko says people don't have enough to eat in Sarajevo so I'm taking some basic clothes and filling the rest of my suitcase with as much food as I can carry. This is serious business, Fair Kate. There are concentration camps like during WWII. From what I can tell so far they're run by Chetniks and other Serbian nationalist groups who don't want an independent Bosnia or any Bosnian Muslims – aka Bosniaks – at all. I've been thinking about your confusion and I wonder if I should try to write a primer to help the average person untangle what's going on and care even though they should care anyway since an entire city is under siege and the Serb forces are bombing maternity hospitals and shooting people in the streets.

I know it's trivial compared to what's happening in Sarajevo but between you, me, and the sublime hot dog smothered in melted Gruyère and wrapped in a baguette that I'm scarfing down from the cart up the street, I'm upset about the situation with Kirby. Right before the shops shut down for August I went to the fromagerie by myself and tried the next cheese on our list – a bouton de culotte from Burgundy. I jotted a few descriptions in a notebook – peppery, goaty – but what's the point without Kirby to argue with? He hates it when I say goaty. Obviously goat cheese is goaty. And it's not just cheeses. I didn't realize how much we discuss every single thing. Street magicians versus street mimes. <u>The Love Bug</u> versus <u>The Apple Dumpling Gang</u>. Plus when I'm with him I don't get hit on. Not that I need a protector, but it can get annoying. This city is Wolf Whistle Central!

I wish I hadn't made him so mad at me. I'm starting to get a little scared too. Since I can't hang out with him, when I got your last letters I went out and bought two of my favorite crêpes – one for me and one for you. I set them on my desk and pretended we were having a meal together while I read your letters. You enjoyed them very much by the way – you told me the sweetness of the onion confit was a perfect complement to the Comté cheese. And you laughed when I read you the riot act. You are not Eliza Doolittle! Just because Old Sven has the market cornered on eloquence – you ARE smart enough for him! You have plenty to teach him too and don't let some Middle-Aged Caftan-Wearing Wannabe Adulteress make you think otherwise.
Adieu from the next great – fingers, toes, and etc. extremities crossed – War Journo Dame,
Frida

8/26/92

Dear Frida,

Hell hath no fury like Seattle during a drought. The radio says this is our worst water shortage in recorded history. Then they play "Raindrops Keep Falling on My Head" like that's funny. It is not funny. It's almost midnight, and I have my door and window propped open with a big fan between them. It isn't helping, especially since Ballard sits on Shilshole Bay. The hot air smells like briny old clamshells.

I'm a brat complaining about the heat when you're probably witnessing horrible things. Concentration camps in 1992? I can't even fathom it. Sven read this T. S. Eliot line to me about how humankind can't bear too much reality. It got me thinking, maybe if we care about every single thing that happens in the world (I mean really care the way we do about our own lives), we'd never get up in the morning. I wish I knew how to think about things like this. Whenever I try it's like a tangled necklace. The more you try to untangle it, the more tangled it gets.

Sorry about the smudges. My hand is drenched in sweat. I'd

use my typewriter, but it's late and everyone's windows are open. I don't want to be rude.

I'm sorry about Kirby, but his feelings are probably hurt. He cares about you. You should apologize when you get back. I bet he feels bad about some of the things he said, too.

It made me smile to imagine having that meal with you. I looked up onion confit. I think I'm going to try and make it so we can have your favorite crêpes "together" in Seattle, too. Thank you for saying I'm smart enough for Sven even though I'm not sure it's true. The other night he got to interview Czeslaw Milosz for Seattle Arts & Lectures. It was a pretty big deal, and afterward we went out to dinner. Mr. Milosz, the store's book buyer and his wife, and Sven and me at a small table in a tiny private room. One of us was a Nobel Prize winner. One of us was Kate Fair.

When Mr. Milosz started comparing what's happening in Yugoslavia now to Poland after WWII, I tried to pay attention, but my anxiety took off like a wild mustang. They all had opinions about the war and what they think will happen if Bill Clinton becomes president, and the next thing I know, "Porcupine Pie" starts up at full volume in my head. I was terrified that if I opened my mouth, I'd shriek, "Vanilla soup, a double scoop please!" They're discussing global politics, and I'm being stalked by Neil Diamond.

They moved on to talking about an artist who refused an NEA grant. You could practically see Sven's brain pulsing. He wasn't afraid to give his opinions to a man like that. I was trying to calm myself down when "Coleslaw Meatloaf" popped into my head. Now for the life of me I couldn't remember Mr. Meatloaf's real name. On top of that, I couldn't stop staring at his eyebrows. They were like two nests stuck above his eyes. I kept imagining birds flying out of them.

I was aware of every particle of dust in the air, and good old Neil won't quit singing about fruity blue cheese in my head. We had him on 8-track when I was a kid, and we practically wore it out in the car. Later when I told Sven how I felt like I was being haunted by "Porcupine Pie," he said he thinks my present is struggling with my past over who I thought I was versus who I am. I used to be a person who accepted everything without question. Now I'm on the path of Socrates who said an unexamined life isn't worth living. I've become a person who examines life. Sometimes being articulated makes me want to curl up on my love seat and read <u>Happy All the Time</u> until the whole world goes away.
Have a very safe day,
Kate

P.S. You're never going to believe this. Caftan Dawn gave Sven a check for $80 made out to her therapist so he can figure out why he's deluding himself about the kind of woman he should be with!

8/29/92

Dear Frida,

This letter is coming to you from the library because the heat wave won't break. I also wanted to check out recent copies of <u>Current</u>. I read two more of Niko's articles. I try to picture you in Sarajevo, but for some reason my imagination can't go there, which is weird because I can ~~totally~~ (old habits die hard) imagine you in Paris eating goat cheese. I know it hasn't even been two weeks since I heard from you. I just wish I could know you're safe.

It's my day off, and I've been here for most of it staying cool. It's a nice place to hide out, balance my checkbook, cruise the card catalog, things like that. It was built in a style called mid-century modern (I'm sure Kirby knows all about it). Some of the walls are these artsy dividers with abstract paintings on them, and there are open spaces filled with stylish chairs and couches. I'm curled up on a black leather one that looks like it's out of a 1960s movie about New York.

I know you won't get my letters until you're back in Paris, and you won't have time to write to me while you're in Sarajevo. I hope it's okay if I keep writing to you. Something ~~strange~~ unsettling happened, and my brain is in full jitter mode. I'd talk to

Sven about it, but sometimes I get tired because he always wants to dissect the deep meaning of things, and I'd call Franny, but I don't want her to worry about me. Don't feel like you have to respond when you eventually read this since you'll have so much on your mind. I just know it will help me sort out my head if I can write it all down to you.

Bumpa finally found a car for me, and Mom came up for the day to drive me over to his place to pick it up. We ended up playing cards so late we stayed the night, and totally spur of the moment, we decided to break in my Chevette with a drive to Toppenish where Bumpa is from. The three of us headed out super early the next morning to get across the pass in time for the maple bars to still be warm at the Cle Elum Bakery. Back when we lived in Eastern Washington, Bumpa would pick up a whole box of them on his way to visit us. They always taste as good as I remember. Sweet with the right hint of salty. We had coffee, too. Talk about a sugar-caffeine buzz. When we got on the road again, the heat picked up. It got hotter and drier the farther inland we drove. $300 doesn't include working air-con so by the time we hit Yakima we had all the windows rolled down. Have I ever told you how pretty my mom is? She has high cheekbones like Bumpa, and I could see the profile of her cute ski jump nose in the side mirror when she stuck her head out the window to smell the sagebrush.

We've never road-tripped just the three of us before. It was fun driving while Mom and Bumpa told old stories. Remember her uncle's ranch where she spent her summers when Bumpa worked on the Brown Bear? It's near Toppenish, and when we reached the turnoff they used to take toward Fort Simcoe, she remembered the time Bumpa let her drive his red-and-white swept-wing Dodge out to the ranch when she was only twelve. And how cool it was she got invited to ride her horse in the all-Indian rodeo parade. I couldn't write anything down because I was driving, but I paid close attention just in case any of it belongs in the novel.

You're probably trying to figure out what's so unsettling about this. I'm getting there. I promise. We started off at the house Bumpa grew up in. It's a yellowish box now, but he says it used to be pure white with French windows and a big sun porch. Then we wandered up the Old West–looking main street to this farm stand. Mom was talking about the cottonwood tree outside her bedroom on the ranch, how peaceful it sounded when the breeze rustled in the leaves,. ~~when I felt like when it was like I suddenly~~ Have you ever heard of an out-of-body experience, Frida? I'm not sure what one is exactly, but I think I had one. I was literally outside my body watching us.

We were sitting on a bench eating peaches warm from the sun. Mom was talking, and Bumpa was smiling in his quiet way. It was like they were connected. Like there was a warm light surrounding them, and I was outside the light. All of a sudden my thoughts sprayed in different directions like fireworks, and Sven's voice, or maybe it was Socrates, was right in the center telling me how an unexamined life isn't worth living, and how come Mom never talks about how hard it was to have divorced parents in the age of Beaver Cleaver, and why didn't Bumpa think about what it felt like to be a single dad back then? It makes sense what you said about Phil Donahue, but it can't be true, can it, I mean about examining life? ~~Just because they don't~~ I don't get how it's so easy for them to be themselves. To just be who they are ~~and not, but for me~~

What's wrong with me? It was a perfect summer day. My fingers were sticky with peach juice, the air was spicy with sagebrush, and Mom was telling the same old family stories. I love our same old stories. Why were they making me feel so melancholy? I physically ached like I was losing something precious. We've always fit together, but I'm changing, Frida. ~~What if I change and I'm so different from~~ I felt so far away from them. It's like I'm stuck inside a tight container and I can't get out but I don't want to get out and I'm fighting to stay in and get out all at the same time. I can't breathe. I thought it would help to write this, but I'm having an anxiety attack right here in the library. How is it possible no one's noticing? There's a lady in the chair across from me looking at an atlas like nothing's wrong. Another lady is chipping gum out of an ashtray. It's like my brain is being dismantled and I have no idea how to put the pieces back together. I need cold water. I need to find the water fountain. I really miss you.

Please stay safe,

Kate

From the new computer of Kate Fair
(It's a hand-me-down gift from my grandma. She and her
husband tried a self-publishing company. Not a success.)

9/4/92

Dear Frida,

I keep telling myself, if something happened to you,
I would know. But how? I looked in a phone book to call
your parents. There are a lot of Rodriguezes in L.A.
I know it's illogical, but every time I hear a story
about Sarajevo on the radio, I listen for your voice.

(I didn't like the way my words looked on the screen so I
printed them out. I don't like them on paper, either. I'm going
back to my pen, but I'll leave the printout section so you can see
what I'm talking about.)

I used to think politicians wanted to do the right thing, but the
U.S. response to Bosnia seems to be all about the coming election.
Will this get me votes? Will that get me votes? Meanwhile, snip-
ers are shooting women hanging laundry in their gardens. It
makes me think how small my troubles are. I'm sorry I was so
melodramatic in my last letter. I'm feeling better. Please be okay.
Your worried friend,
Kate

9/12/92

Dear Frida,

Autumn is finally rolling in. There were hints of coolness when the sun went down last night, and I woke up to a drizzly rain on the skylights. When I opened my window, I could tell the air is ready to be done with the heat. It's that back-to-school feeling that makes you nostalgic in an aching kind of way.

Two weeks is more than up. Are you still in Sarajevo? Dumb question since if you are you can't answer since you won't get this letter until you're back. I don't know if you're safe, but I have to keep writing to you like you are, like everything's normal, whatever that means. I know the world is miserable, but good things are happening right now, and I feel like I'm going to explode because I haven't shared them with you.

I was promoted to our special orders department. When a customer asks for a book we can't get from our distributors or the publishers we have accounts with, our department hunts it down. We're like book detectives. We have this massive resource called <u>Books in Print</u>. It weighs in at 1,287 pages. Take that, <u>Larousse</u>

<u>Gastronomique</u>! We process more than a thousand special orders a month. The department is run by Mae. She's an artist who makes sculptures out of stripped mass markets, and to call her a tough boss is an understatement. She's not mean or anything. She just wants the job done right, and she chose ME! She put me in charge of something as important as tracking down special requests. She thinks I can do the job right!

Please don't think I think this is more important than Sarajevo. It's confusing knowing about what's going on over there when my life keeps going on over here like over there doesn't exist. Does that make sense? Does it make sense that I cried when I read about that bomb hitting the busload of orphans, but the same day I felt happy about a short story I started? I got to thinking about trying short stories after I read Laura Kalpakian's "Sonnet." It made me wonder if maybe it's easier to try an idea in a story because if it doesn't work you haven't lost a year writing an entire novel. (Plus you can pack a punch with a short story, like in "Sonnet" when the daughter is deciding whether or not to give her dad the cologne. I won't spoil it for you since I'm sending it to you.)

Once I finish, Sven's going to help me sell it. He has lots of contacts through all the authors he knows. It's about a young woman who works in a bookstore. She's obsessed with writing about her family, and even though she isn't sure what she wants to say, she keeps writing anyway. I got the idea from Madeleine L'Engle's <u>A Circle of Quiet</u>. She wrote, "Inspiration does not always precede the act of writing; it often follows it." Sven says I'm doing something called metafiction. He's trying to get me to read Jorge Luis Borges, but I'll stick with Madeleine for now.

Things are going great for Sven, too. He finished his novel, and his agent thinks he could be the next Updike. How amazing is that? We had dinner at Lombardi's to celebrate being Special Order Royalty and Sir Updike the Second. Afterward we headed to Bumbershoot, this big arts and literary festival that happens at the end of every summer at Seattle Center. It was still blazing hot. All the flags in front of the international fountain drooped like limp dishrags, but no one cared. The sky was pearly blue from the city lights. There was this Latin band, and the whole crowd was dancing. There must have been hundreds of us. Sven was waving his hands in the air and spinning around and laughing. I love it when he gives his Big Thoughts a rest. I can literally see the tension leave him. He smiles differently and

Ring-ring goes my phone. Be right back!

Bumpa had a stroke. Your letter is back at the apartment. One of the nurses gave me this notebook. I'm in a hospital in Kirkland. Dad wanted to stay, but Mom made him go home to take care of the dog and because he has a big meeting with the governor tomorrow about some transportation funding. She and Franny are asleep in chairs by Bumpa's bed. He's sleeping, too. There's a green glow coming from somewhere and an eerie humming sound from the monitors. He woke up for a while earlier, and when he saw us, he smiled. Franny said, "Hey Bumpa, that's a dapper zebra-striped shirt you're wearing." We waited for him to say something like, "Golly, those sure are spiffy orange-and-purple plaid boots you have on." But when he opened his mouth, no words came out. Just this garbled sound. He must have been able to hear himself because he looked confused. His eyes started to move around the room, and I guess he realized something was wrong because he got this panicked look. Mom held his good hand. That seemed to help, but if she let go, his hand flailed around like she was a life raft. As soon as she held it again, he calmed down. She's holding it now even though they're both asleep. The room smells awful. Like someone left lilies behind and they're starting to rot. The doctor told Mom the stroke is serious. Maybe Bumpa will never talk again. I don't get it. How can a brain change so fast like that? I found the pay phone and called

Sven. I told him Bumpa wasn't done telling me his stories. Do you know what he said? "That's the curse of life, my love. The inevitability of disappointment." SHUT UP SHUT UP SHUT UP! Bumpa is the kindest man I've ever known. He doesn't deserve this. Frida, I don't think I'm okay.

PART TWO

In the beginning I was so young and such a stranger to myself I hardly existed. I had to go out into the world and see it and hear it and react to it, before I knew at all who I was, what I was, what I wanted to be.

—Mary Oliver, *Upstream: Selected Essays*

FRIDA RODRIGUEZ ... ~~EN ROUTE~~ *broken*

October 3, 1992
Paris, France

Dear Kate,

I should get down on my knees in front of invincible Martha Gellhorn and gutsy old Claudia from <u>Moon Tiger</u> and beg their forgiveness for letting them down. I've been back in Paris for a month. I can hardly go outside without crying – the city is beautiful and tranquil and I can buy buttery Brie any time I want without being shot at. I've been too depressed to open your letters but I need to. I miss you so much. It's not fair with everyone in Sarajevo living on rations, but I'm going to buy us a greasy choucroute and gorge on tangy cabbage and smoky sausage while I read your words. I understand how spoiled I am now, Kate. We're all spoiled. None of us gross selfish twentysomethings has any idea how easy we have it. Have you and Sven figured out the meaning of life by now? I hope so. After Sarajevo I wonder if there's any meaning at all. You'll understand when you read my notebook.

Frida

Sarajevo Notebook
Frida Rodriguez, WJD (War Journo Dame)

Time to get serious:

1) No run-on sentences.
2) Cool it with the dashes.
3) Use commas.

8/23, Day 1
2 p.m., Holiday Inn Sarajevo

Fair Kate,

I'm here. Sarajevo. How can it feel so unreal when this hotel room is very, very real with a big pane window crisscrossed with duct tape to keep it from spraying glass everywhere? I'm using one of my Reporter's Note Books to write to you since I forgot stationery and the only things on our desk are cigarette burns and this isn't the place for a jaunt to the five-and-dime. Run-on sentences already!. Ugh. Another issue I need to deal with. I have a journalism degree for crying out loud. I do know how to write without exclamation marks.

When the plane's wheels shuddered on the tarmac, the sun looked like a ~~globe~~ lozenge of melting ivory in the smoky sky. How's that? You're so good at describing things. I don't want to be a just-the-facts-ma'am journalist. I need to practice descriptions so my readers can feel what it was like to fly in on Maybe Airlines – not the real name – that's what the War Journos call it.

You'd think my whole body would be pulsing with adrenaline, especially after the plane did a nose-dive on its descent to avoid being shot down, but I felt like I'd been drugged with anesthesia when Niko met me at the airport. Remember how you wrote about feeling too close to yourself and too far away at the same time? In Paris Niko told me the road from the airport to the city is called Sniper Alley. It sounded thrilling on the banks of the Seine after a bottle of Beaujolais. So <u>Year of Living Dangerously</u> when Mel Gibson and Sigourney Weaver blast through that military roadblock. But if somebody asked me to describe an apocalypse, it's the drive to the hotel. Destroyed buildings and burned-out cars everywhere.

Niko drives a Land Rover nicknamed – get this – Mr. Kotter. He raced through the empty street and when I told him I didn't expect it to be so quiet, he said, "Don't let the lulls fool you, Cub, you're on a highway straight to hell and you never know when a shell has your name on it." He was full-on pedal to the metal but he sounded so nonchalant I think I'm still waiting for his words to sink in.

War Journos, diplomats, and aid workers stay at the Holiday Inn. It looks like a gargantuan cube of Emmental. Sallow yellow and pocked with bullet holes. At the back entrance you can drive right into the underground parking garage. Niko gunned it and squealed down the ramp to make it harder for the snipers to shoot us. Can you believe I'm writing sentences like that? He hauled my bag into the massive atrium lobby. Tarps are stretched over the windows where the glass was blown out. War journos sat around slurping coffee, and a few of them tapped on those new little portable computers like we're in a sci-fi movie.

My mind was in overdrive trying to observe everything.

- A guy wearing a helmet while he ate Froot Loops of all things!.

- A woman with frizzy blond hair and a chunky turquoise necklace at a piano playing Carole King's "I Feel the Earth Move." How's that for cynical?

- Niko giving me duct tape and a Sharpie so I could write my name and blood type and stick it on my flak jacket. Yes I have a flak jacket.

Up in the room I heard a muffled cracking sound. Sniper's Corner is out front. Niko said it's the most dangerous intersection in the city, but don't worry, Cub, you'll get used to it. ~~On the Seine it was all about thoughtful explanations and lingering kisses, but apparently Sarajevo is terse words and a quick dry peck on the temple that made me feel~~ Seriously? I'm in a city under siege Kate, and I'm thinking about kisses! What's wrong with me?

I think Niko's preoccupied because <u>Time</u> beat him to jolting the world with their cover story about the concentration camps. He's been working on a guard at one of the camps for a while. The guy claims he secretly took pictures inside. Niko's still trying to gain his trust. That's why he's out right now and I'm not. That and a tanker came for the hotel cistern. Someone has to stay and fill our bathtub to the brim since there's no telling when the next delivery will be. The Serbs cut off water supplies and most of the city's electricity too although the hotel has its own generator.

Hotel Room Rule #1: Don't stand by the windows – I swear I've never paid this much attention to windows in my whole life. I'm sitting in a corner with my notebook propped on my knees, hypnotized by the steady crack and boom of shelling down in the streets. Why do I feel so remote writing those words? Those bombs are anything but remote. This is what I'm meant

to do, isn't it, Kate? ~~But something's not doesn't feel~~
No – I can say anything to you. Something doesn't
feel right. I wish I'd packed <u>The Face of War</u>. I need
Martha right now.

<u>10 p.m., Holiday Inn Sarajevo</u>

Dear Kate,

After a few hours in the room I realized I didn't
know when Niko was coming back. I was getting a
serious case of leg cramps from huddling in the corner so I wandered down to the lobby. I saw a guy
reading one of the copies of the <u>Tribune</u> Niko brought
back from Paris. Niko told me, "The journos like to
check up on the rest of the world, Cub, to make sure
they chose the best war." How sobering is that? It
really is a century of wars, isn't it? Did I mention
Niko gave me the nickname Cub for cub reporter in
Paris? ~~It sounded sweet when we were there, but
when he called me Cub in front of another journo at
dinner tonight I could feel myself shrinking and I
hate the way I feel like~~

I've never been so hyperaware of every single
thing happening in relation to how it makes me feel.
This isn't about my feelings! This isn't about me! – Or

myself! – Or I for that matter! – but I don't know how
to get rid of Me-Myself-I and even if I did I don't feel
like Me-Myself-I right now which makes me wonder
who Me-Myself-I is since I thought I knew but apparently I didn't which is a whole other issue and now
isn't the time for that kind of navel-gazing and this
might be my worst run-on sentence ever.

What I should be writing about is how $82 a
night gets you three meals a day in this hotel. A couple journos were wearing their flak jackets to eat, but
the waiters wear suit jackets and bow ties like they
work at the Ritz. At dinner in the safe, windowless
dining room there was red wine and braised steaks
and decent crêpes with chocolate sauce for dessert.
The forks and knives have the Olympics symbol em-
bossed on them – the hotel was built for the 1984
Olympics – and I wondered if anyone else felt as horrible as I did enjoying good food while the rest of the
city lives off food aid rations. There's a rumor some of
it has expiration dates from the 1970s!

The frizzy blonde was back at the piano. When we
walked in, she started playing "You're So Vain" and
Niko's friend, a hairy British guy whose name is actually Harry, said, "Look out pretty boy, Bobbie's
gunning for you." Niko laughed and said, "Water under the bridge." Great! A jealous ex who happens to

be great at her job. I've seen her reporting on Sky TV. Not what Me-Myself-I needs right now.

I thought Niko would introduce me around during dinner but he got into one of those conversations that feels like it's been going on for years and I couldn't find a way to jump in. I'm thinking we'll talk once we're back in the room. We'll lie in bed and I'll tell him how disconnected I'm feeling and ask him if that's normal for a newbie and he'll say yes, Cub, absolutely, and I'll feel better and they covered a century of wars together and lived happily ever after. Ha! Sixty seconds and he was out like a light. Now I'm sitting in the dark with Serb forces hunkered down in the hills surrounding the city. Our room isn't on the worst side, but I can still see when they launch a mortar shell. There's a quick flash like a white carnation. They took over buildings too and I can actually see the red laser beams they use to track people in the streets and even though I read all my WJDs front to back and all over again ~~I feel like it makes me sick to I'm not I can't even~~

Midnight, Holiday Inn Sarajevo

I can't sleep. Confession: I need to tell you something but I'm afraid you'll be disappointed in me. But if I don't tell you, I'll be disappointed in myself because we're not the kind of friends who keep things from each other. I'm scared, Kate. Not like when you're watching a horror movie waiting for Freddy Krueger to jump out but deep in my bones scared. That drive from the airport. A highway straight to hell rattling with spent shell casings. The parliament building across the road is still smoking from being bombarded a few days ago. It sounds like the never-ending grand finale at a fireworks show out there. I knew it was bad here – really bad – but this bad? How could it be this bad? If it's this bad – and it is this bad – the world would stop it. But the world isn't stopping it. I'm terrified of getting shot. I'm terrified of bombs. I'm no dummy. But it's not just that. People live here. This is their home. I can hear – I can feel! – bombs falling on them <u>right now</u> while I write to you. Who is Frida Rodriguez to think her words can have any impact when veteran journalists are reporting every day for the BBC, <u>NYT</u>, <u>London Times</u>, AP, Reuters, CNN – you name it, even the Vatican has a radio correspondent here – and no one outside this country gives a damn because if they did this wouldn't be happening.

8/24, Day 2
Noon, National Library

Dear Kate,

It turns out the postal service is out of commission so I can't send you anything I've written – probably for the best, it's so pathetic. Niko's back with his guard from the camp. Before he left he brought me to the national library – which is also the university library – to see if I could find any students – get their perspective. He says a War Journo's job is to keep talking to people until you find a story that needs to be told. I asked him how will I know? He said you'll know, Cub, you'll just know. Easy for him to say.

Even though a peace conference started in London, the Serb forces are ramping up their attacks. On the way here the shelling was nonstop. The library isn't far from the hotel, but we had to zigzag down Zmaja od Bosne – Sniper Alley. When I got out of Mr. Kotter, I saw an old woman on a street corner gripping a girl's wrist. They were pressed into the doorway of a building to keep from being exposed. The girl looked like she was kindergarten age. She had pale red hair and pale pink skin and she was wearing a powder-blue Smurfette t-shirt. The old woman darted out dragging the girl as fast as she could down the street until they were safe behind a steel shipping container set up for a shield. People don't get caught in crossfire here Kate. There is no crossfire. Every single person is a target. There are ropes tied to lampposts to pull yourself to safety if you're shot! Is that a story that needs to be told?

I got to the library a while ago and I've been sitting here paralyzed. I blame the building for not knowing there's a war going on. It's a painfully beautiful contrast to the ugliness in the streets. ~~I wonder what Kirby would have to say about a place like this in the middle of a war. I'm furious at myself for not making up with him before I left. It feels like a part of me~~ The architecture is a stunning combination of mosque and cathedral with arches and lacy woodwork and sunlight filtering through stained glass. You know that library smell? The sweet dust of old paper. It makes what's going on outside feel impossible even though I hear it plain as day. How do the Serb forces have so many mortars?

Since it's summer and there's a war going on I'm not sure if any classes are in session, but I found a big reading room – it looks like it used to be an auditorium – with a few students studying and hanging out at some tables. It's weird how they look like they could be in L.A. Reading and whispering and even laughing. It's unsettling to hear laughter when a little girl who loves Smurfette is running for her life in the streets. When the students leave here today, they'll run for their lives too. ~~I could never laugh if I lived in a place like this. I'd feel too~~

Snap! Out! Of! It! No one cares what Me-Myself-I could never do!

Martha Gellhorn.

Be Martha Gellhorn.

Martha Gellhorn observed and reported.

Observe and report!

Okay Kate, here I go, I'm going to pick a table. Got it! That one over there. There are two students. Joan Jett Hair and Translucent Girl. Joan Jett Hair is talking intensely about the book in her hand. Hold still so I can see what you're reading. That's it. Steady. <u>Something Totalitarianism</u> by Hannah Somebody. The book is in English but they're not speaking English but they must know English to read a book in English. Joan Jett just looked me square in the eye. I nodded. I should go over there and talk to them. I should ask them what stories need to be told. I'm getting up.

<u>2 p.m., National Library</u>

What's the matter with me? I stood up, turned around, and walked in the opposite direction. I told myself I was going to see if I could find an English section for a book by the same author so I'd have a reason to strike up a conversation. I found a librarian whose English was pretty good but something obviously got lost in the translation – I ended up spending the past hour reading a beat-up old British copy of Little Women.

9 p.m., Holiday Inn Sarajevo

Dear Kate,

Back at the hotel Niko took a nap and slept through dinner and he's still sleeping. I didn't feel like waking him up because then we'd have to talk about how I wasted my day, and I couldn't go down to the restaurant by myself. I don't get it. Frida Rodriguez has never been afraid to walk into a crowded room alone. It's not who I am but it doesn't matter who I am because I stayed upstairs. Sunset rinsed the sky with milky pink nectar and I watched the hills transform into a dusky garden blooming with phosphorescent carnations. How's that for a Kate Fair description? I didn't have much for lunch and my stomach started to rumble. Get this – I felt sorry for myself. Seriously! I'm not starving. The people who live in Sarajevo ration food and cook in makeshift woodstoves because there's no electricity most of the time – not like here in the Important Journo Hotel with its Big Generator. I'm hungry that's all and I don't have to be because I could walk downstairs and have beef stew but I don't want beef stew I want Mom's chiles rellenos and oh my God I'm crying for chiles rellenos.

I can't breathe. Slow down slooooow dowwwwwn but when I slow down I think about the pale girl in the Smurfette shirt and is that why I've got chiles rellenos in my head? When I was her age I asked Mom how farmers grow chiles with cheese in them. She said why don't we find out and we planted some Anaheims and one day Dad called me outside and there on the vine were two chiles with strips of cheese inside. I was deliriously happy. It took me years to figure out Dad snuck outside and slit the peppers and tucked the cheese in. They still laugh about it. They still don't know I'm here. What kind of person goes to war and doesn't tell her parents? What is that little girl going to remember if she lives long enough to have childhood memories? Unless her mom never lets her out of the house again – even then – shells hit houses and kill children all the time here. All it takes is one piece of shrapnel. Does she like to read? I hope she likes to read. I hope she has books for escape. I escaped today and I can't believe it – I stole <u>Little Women</u> from the library. I couldn't bear the thought of being back in this room without a book. What was I thinking not bringing a book? I've never traveled anywhere without a book. I stole a book in the middle of a war!

8/25, Day 3
1 p.m., National Library

What a day so far! You'd be proud of me, Fair Kate. Who knows what kind of magic happened while I was sleeping. Who cares? I've been purged. I leaped out of bed ready to ditch Pity Party Me-Myself-I and take my War Journo Dameness and some well-placed commas back to the library and track down my very own story that needs to be told. And return Little Women. I donned my oh so fashionable – and heavy! – flak jacket and gave Niko a surprise when he sauntered into the dining room and found me deep in conversation with Hairy Harry over bacon and eggs.

When I told Hairy Harry where I was going, he gave me the Reader's Digest condensed version of the Austro-Hungarian occupation of Bosnia and Herzegovina. That's the country's whole name, by the way. During the late 1800s the occupiers built a new city hall – it eventually became this library in 1951 – in neo-Moorish style. The architect got his ideas from trips to Cairo, and even though the new rulers were Catholic, the building recognized the country's Muslim heritage. Hairy Harry says that mentality has been the beauty of Bosnia and now its curse. It's the most multiethnic republic in Yugoslavia, and that's the last thing any staunch nationalist wants. I took careful notes and asked smart questions. I'm here, Fair Kate! I'm finally here!

I told Niko I wanted to go to the library again, and he asked if I found my story. Not yet is what I said then. What a difference a few hours can make! But let me take it slowly as I sit in this sanctum belles-lettres, the hushed percussion of mortars no match for the complex lives inside this fortress of books.

Back in the library, taking off my flak jacket and sitting down in a corner to figure out my strategy, the first person I saw was Joan Jett Hair in a David Bowie t-shirt and acid-washed jeans. She walked right up to me, stuck out her hand and said, "Hello, I am Lejla. You are American?"

How did she know? I have brown skin. People back in America don't even think I'm American. She pointed at my feet and said – in flawless English – "I think Americans love brand new white tennis shoes." I told her I never wear tennis shoes but I bought these in Paris in case I have to run fast here. This made her laugh. "You are an aid worker?" she asked. I shook my head but before I could tell her I'm a WJD she held up her hand and said, "I will guess. You are CIA?" I thought she was joking. She wasn't. Doctor? No. UN official? No. It was disorienting because her makeup was gloomy and goth but her curiosity was warm. Finally she guessed journalist and I told her I'm trying to find a story that needs to be told.

You should have seen the look on her face. She flung out her arms and declared, "It is here!" She told me the library has almost two million books. Muslim, Catholic, Jewish, Orthodox. Bosnian, Croatian, Serbian. It was like what Hairy Harry told me. Lejla said they live peacefully together under the same roof the way the people of Sarajevo had been living together under the same sky. They're proof that harmony is possible but the nationalists don't want harmony. They want ethnic purity. The shelling outside sounded like it was getting even worse. She ran her fingers through her hair. The spikes stood up like candle flames. She told me she kissed her first boyfriend next to ancient Ottoman manuscripts. She said, "A Catholic and I am Muslim! I think no one wants the story of how Bosnians get along. They only want the story of how we hate each other because people love stories about hate. I watch <u>Dallas</u>."

My mind was leapfrogging all over the place when she told me about reading her first English-language book in the library on a Sunday morning while her mom worked as a cleaner. Her cousin used to send her books from Washington, D.C. She asked if I'd heard of <u>Are You There God? It's Me, Margaret.</u>? Did I gasp? You bet I did, Fair Kate. Every girl I knew read that book but I never imagined girls reading it in other countries. Lejla told me Margaret taught her what a period was. Same for me. Poor Mom when I demanded to know if it was true. Ask her about roasted chayotes and she'll talk until the sun comes up, but mention Aunt Flo and all of a sudden she's late for a meeting!

Lejla said, "Growing up I heard women say 'I have <u>it</u>.' What did they have? No one would tell me. But I think Judy Blume is a straight shooter." Lejla loves books as much as we do. It's incredible how many American authors she's read. Mark Twain, Pearl S. Buck, Edgar Allan Poe. She grinned and looked around and whispered, "I am naughty." Whenever she finishes reading a book, she draws a purple butterfly inside the back cover. There are eight purple butterflies inside her Margaret book. There are purple butterflies all over the library. Lejla swept her arm toward the table where her translucent friend was sitting and said, "Irena gets mad at me. She says I am a vandal. She is my best friend. All our lives we were Yugoslavian but now the Serbs say she is Serb

Orthodox and I am Bosnian Muslim, and that we should hate each other for this. We don't buy their partisan garbage."

My whole body trembled. Niko's right. I just knew. This story – the story of what Sarajevo is rather than what it isn't – it needs to be told. I asked Lejla if I could interview her. She was ecstatic. She told me how everyone wants bullets and bombs. Or a dead child because they think dead children will stop a war but when in history has a dead child ever stopped a war? Men in power don't care about dead children. If they did there would be no wars at all. She said if I was going to interview her I should interview Irena too – they both studied in London so her English is as fluent as Lejla's – but don't let Irena talk about Bono because when she starts in on <u>Rattle and Hum</u> it's impossible to shut her up. Then she had to go help her mom and she invited me to an underground café later for our first interview. This is it, Fair Kate. I'm sure of it!

<u>8/27, Day 5</u>
<u>4 a.m., Holiday Inn Sarajevo</u>

I wanted to write to you last night before bed but I was dead tired. Then I woke up wide awake and realized I couldn't go back to sleep unless I told you what happened even though who knows when you'll get this letter so why does it feel like it matters if I write to you ASAP and not tomorrow? I snuck down to the kitchen. I thought the bakers were ignoring me snooping in the cupboards, but while I was heating water for the Nescafé I brought with me, one of them tapped my shoulder. I turned around. I must have looked the way I felt because she squeezed my arm and handed me a warm roll dotted with gems of plum jam. It takes my breath away how someone can be so kind to a stranger in the middle of all this misery.

It's eerie here in the lobby. I'm the only one awake. There's glass in piles in the corners. The hotel was hit on Tuesday too. The journos say it's the worst shelling so far. Is it only Thursday? Was it only two nights ago when I met up with Lejla and Irena at the under-ground café? I thought they meant it was secret or maybe subversive but it was just literally underground. A few university students turned a cellar near the li-brary into a meeting place. It made me think about what Martha wrote – how a basement is more desir-able in a time of war than a time of peace. The walls were plastered with posters. David Hasselhoff, Michael Jackson, and John Lennon, as well as a few Bosnian celebrities – I assume – that I didn't recognize and some old promotional ads for the 1984 Olympics. Along with tables and chairs, cots were stacked in a corner in case anyone needed to stay the night. I wish I'd known to bring something. Everyone showed up with thermoses of tea or bottles of liquor. No electricity – just candles and a moody guy whose Simon & Garfunkel guitar playing did not match his Duran Duran mullet.

A girl had a pack of Drina cigarettes and she rationed them out while everyone tried to explain Tito to me – it's amazing how many students here speak such fluent English. They told me when he became president of Yugoslavia he said he wanted to create a federal republic made up of equal nations and nationalities – things got heated with an argument about politics in theory versus reality, and the cigarette girl declared the only people who believe in benevolent dictatorships are people who've never lived in a benevolent dictatorship. Don't ask me how but this led to questions about <u>Murphy Brown</u> and the American Way. I blame the fiery plum brandy being passed around.

I understood why they created this place. It felt almost normal. But normal can't be relied on in a war zone, Kate. Mullet was strumming "Bridge Over Troubled Water" with everyone singing along when a guy ran down the stairs and yelled, "They're bombing the library!" We looked at each other like he was speaking Latin. The next thing I knew we all flew up the stairs.

The first people outside turned around and shouted, "Go back! Go back!" I stumbled into the person behind me, but I could still see out the door. Flaming meteors striped the sky, exploding into the dome of the library. We should have retreated into the cellar, but the shock paralyzed us. Grenades sounded like they were shredding the night. I heard Lejla scream Irena's name. I pushed forward and saw Irena running. I tried to grab Lejla's arm, but she jerked away. I caught up to them in a doorway opposite the library. Irena gasped something in her own language and then in English. "They stopped, thank God they stopped."

We thought it was over, but it wasn't. "Flames!" Lejla cried, pointing up. A bright orange wave thrashed out of the library. We looked at each other, but what could we do? A tanker finally arrived, and some men aimed a hose. A single hose, Kate! There was only one truck because the Serb forces bombed the surrounding streets so nothing could get through. They severed the pipelines. The river was right there, but the men couldn't fill the tank fast enough. The flames grew, and the night smelled like the end of the world. It wasn't just the library. The entire city was on fire. I couldn't breathe, Kate. I can't breathe.

Somehow I was in a chain of people. Firemen and librarians raced into the library and passed books out to us. The fire was far above us, but cinders flew and it scorched every particle of air. It tasted like chemicals, and I couldn't cover my mouth because I needed my hands for the books. When I rubbed my eyes, the soot felt like needles. The fire sounded like wax paper crackling in my ears, and there were cracks like a whip. I thought it was the flames, but it was gunshots. Kate, the snipers were shooting at human beings trying to save books. I was a human being trying to save books.

I can't remember how, but we were huddled back in the doorway again. I don't know how Niko found me. He drove Irena and Lejla home before we went back to the hotel. I smelled like a bonfire. I stared at the bathtub. All that water felt obscene. I let myself use a small ration but there's still smoke inside me. I smell it every time I breathe. It's under my skin.

I slept through most of the morning. When I woke up, Niko was gone. The desk clerk gave me a note from Lejla. It had an address on it. I asked Hairy Harry for a ride in his battered VW Golf that is most definitely not sniper-proof. Fire still raged out the library's windows, and gray smoke eclipsed the sun. Butterflies floated in the sooty air. Hundreds of Lejla's butterflies dancing like lace across the dimmed daylight. I was sure I was losing my mind until I got out of the car and saw they weren't butterflies. They were books, Kate. Downy fragments of the library's precious books. I held up my hand and a wisp of paper settled on my palm. It was warm on my skin like a brush of sunlight. Then poof. It was ash. Gone.

Do you remember how we wrote it's the words that will last? Is it true if something like this can happen? Words living together in harmony under the same roof – incinerated in a single gust of hate.

6 p.m., Holiday Inn Sarajevo

I keep getting interrupted and losing track of time. Even though I'm writing Day 1, Day 2, it's hard to keep things straight. I was telling you how I got out of Hairy Harry's car in a soft rain of butterflies. That feels like a century ago. Hairy Harry dropped me off at a small house with timber beams and a clay tile roof. It would have looked like a fairy tale cottage if the windows weren't blown out. All the windows on the block are gone, and the house across the street has a crater in its roof with part of the wall exposed so you can see yellow cabbage roses on the wallpaper. An old woman answered the door. I followed her down a dark hall into the smoky light of a garden. Ash from the books dusted a linden tree the way ash from wild-fires dusts our lemon and guava trees back home.

Lejla jumped up from a chair. I know I just met her, but she looked like a completely different person from the girl in the library talking about Judy Blume. On the surface she was still the same, smudged raccoon eyeliner and the torn <u>Flashdance</u> collar of her Blondie t-shirt slipping off her shoulder. But a layer of her youth had been singed away. I wondered if I seemed different to her. I felt different.

She grabbed my hand and asked, "You will still tell our story?" My skin prickled. I felt helpless. The way she and Irena were looking at me, I could see it in their eyes how much they needed someone – me – to save them. Before I could say a word a child ran past me and jumped onto Irena's lap. I'm never speechless, but my vocal cords froze. You won't believe this. Remember the pale redhead in the Smurfette t-shirt? The little girl I saw running in the street. It was her! Maybe Irena thought I wasn't answering Lejla's question because I had changed my mind. Fiercely, she said, "The Serbs think to bomb the library can erase our bonds. We will not allow it! You must tell the world about people like us for the sake of children like my niece Branka."

She clutched the girl. I couldn't believe Smurfette was right in front of me. I was still speechless and

Lejla jumped in and said, "Not all Serbs are the enemy. This is important. It is the nationalists who are using the excuse of ancient rivalries. That is not who we are today. There were Croats in the café last night. The guitar player is Czech and Slovenian." She talked fast like she was afraid I'd cut her off, telling me how Serb nationalists use fanaticism to pit neighbors against neighbors while UN peacekeepers are as useless as rocks and George Bush says America will support the new government of Bosnia and Herzegovina with full diplomatic relations but Bill Clinton calls that a lukewarm response and what do I think? Am I voting for Clinton?

I haven't even been following the election in my own country. I'm only barely beginning to understand Bosnia. I'm still shaking from the library. I'm in over my head and I was terrified because this is more than just a story that needs to be told. I knew with my whole heart – this is it, Kate – this is <u>MY</u> story. I want this. I want to make a difference and I'm afraid nothing will make a difference. The city is smoldering in every direction. If no one's coming to their rescue after the last bombardments, what good will it do to tell the world about two best friends in Sarajevo who crossed the ethnic divide and liked to snack on Smoki puffs while they watched <u>The Fresh Prince of Bel-Air</u>?

The garden was silent. Without power there were no radios or TVs, but what unnerved me most was no shelling. That's how fast a person can get used to it. I was already more aware of when it was absent than when it was present. Ash rustled in the leaves, and I wanted to say something reassuring but my brain was clogged with butterflies. My tongue was gummy with soot. I crawled through the debris in my thoughts until I found Martha and asked her what she would say right now, and she frowned at me and waved her menthol and said, "Why are you asking me? This isn't my story. What do you want to know?"

Remember that primer I said I was going to write? It's so complex here, Kate. The same word can mean a nationality or an ethnicity, and a person can have one ethnicity and another nationality – and ethnicity, nationality, and religion too – it all plays a part in what side you're on. Plus I still don't know if I'm using the right terms for the different kinds of weapons. But what did Me-Myself-I really want to know? I looked from rock 'n' roll Lejla in her combat boots to ethereal Irena in her gauzy hippie dress and said, "Tell me about an Orthodox Serb and a Muslim Bosnian being best friends."

In the haze of an exposed garden in a city under siege they glanced at each other uncertainly. But it was like they couldn't stop themselves. Like they had to tell me everything as fast as they could before they lost the chance. They were born three weeks apart and grew up on the same street, and it seems like there's nothing they didn't share. A love for books by an author called Nasiha Kapidžić-Hadžić when they were girls, and an intense Agatha Christie phase during one summer youth camp for Tito's Pioneers – think Girl Scouts with a Communist twist. Their favorite band was Zabranjeno Pušenje until Irena discovered U2. "It was our first fight," Lejla teased Irena. Irena went off on a tangent about the music video for "In the Name of Love," and then they were arguing about the obligations of music and Irena insisted Zabranjeno Pušenje's politics weren't big enough and Lejla insisted they taught young Yugoslavians to think about social issues and the next thing I knew they were howling with laughter about how they spent the entire 1984 Winter Olympics hanging around the entrance to the Olympic Village begging everyone who went in to get them Katarina Witt's autograph.

The Serbs have no idea. This war that's supposed to divide them is making them even closer. I knew it was illogical when a shell could crash down on us at any second, but I thought – they're so lucky.

The more they talked, the more the war disappeared. Smoke masked the sun, butterflies dissolved mid-flight, and their past was as alive as the present. Their past is their weapon against the present and the enemy can go to hell if it thinks it can wipe out that past.

Irena and her sister – Branka's mom – live together with their grandma. Irena's sister is a surgeon so she's rarely home anymore. The shelling started up again, and Irena's grandma begged us to come inside, but Irena said they were tired of hiding in the back corners of rooms all the time. Like me right now sitting on the floor in the back corner of my hotel room trying to imagine what it must feel like to go from one life to another overnight. Not figuratively. One beautiful spring day they were in a café dissecting a new American album called <u>Nevermind</u> over bottles of apricot Fructal and Schweppes. The next day they were running from snipers in the streets. It doesn't make sense.

Here's my problem, Kate. I'm trying, I am, but I can't imagine what it feels like. How is that possible when I'm in the middle of it, but I don't feel like I'm in the middle of it – I feel like I'm outside it – even when we were passing the books and the fire was raging and the snipers were shooting – I found out they killed a woman, a librarian, Aida Buturović – I could have died like her, I could die like anyone else here, but I'm not like anyone else here because this isn't my home. So how can I understand what it feels like to lose what they're losing, and if I can't understand then how can I write about it? I need to stop now before I spiral, I can't spiral, they deserve more from me.

Almost Midnight, Holiday Inn Sarajevo

I can't sleep. I can't stop thinking about the library. It surprised me. It wasn't like what we learned in school about life behind the Iron Curtain when we were growing up. I thought everything here would be drab with nothing to read but Communist propaganda. But that beautiful library housed hundreds of thousands of rare books and manuscripts, the national archives, and the university's collections. The Serb forces fired phosphorus shells so hot they melted the lead into the stone walls. One moment it was a cultural stronghold. The next a charred shell filled with ash and burned stones. Lejla says the goal is to erase the entire Muslim existence in Bosnia. Irena used that word too. I have this picture in my head of a giant eraser sweeping across a whole population leaving a big blank swath. Erase. A nothing word – an everything word – depending on who's using it or how ~~or~~ ~~if~~ I'm chasing an idea around in my head but I can't catch it.

I was hoping to talk to Niko about all of this at dinner tonight thinking maybe he could help me map out an article for <u>Alt News L.A.</u> but he was telling Hairy Harry and frizzy blond piano-playing Bobbie that his guard finally showed him photos and it's worse than he imagined which is saying a lot considering everything he's seen in his career. What could I do? Interrupt Niko's eyewitness to atrocities to tell him I have this gut feeling that what happened to the library is directly connected to every horrific thing happening in the camps? That every burned book is connected to every sniper and bomb. That everything happening to the lives of Lejla and Irena comes down to words and who is using them and how. Nationalism. Muslim. Erase.

<u>8/28, Day 6</u>
<u>8 p.m., Holiday Inn Sarajevo</u>

You'd never know there was a peace agreement in London. The shelling is incessant, but if the Serbs think they're winning, they need to meet Lejla and Irena. When I went back to the house, they were their own army of two on a mission. Their uniforms? A Clash t-shirt for Lejla and a filmy Stevie Nicks skirt for Irena. In the garden they set up three tables with three manual typewriters. They already have a plan. With the library destroyed, the university students lost invaluable resources. Lejla and Irena are going to make lists of what individual students need. Three typewriters and who knows how many students but I wasn't about to argue. A lot of students studied abroad so they'll ask them for their contacts at those universities. Then they're going to reach out to professors, libraries, and research centers to track down books. I don't know how this is going to happen without a postal service or phones or even electricity, but if anyone can do it, it's these two.

<u>8/29, Day 7</u>
<u>10 p.m., Holiday Inn Sarajevo</u>

I figured I can get some attention for Lejla and Irena's project by pitching articles to college newspapers around the U.S. We decided I'd talk to the students who speak English – get their stories to weave into my pitches. Sounds simple enough but when I woke up this morning for my first day of interviews, my courage was nowhere to be found. It took me half an hour to force myself out of bed and another half hour to brush my teeth. The more I think about writing about this experience, the more I'm discovering the inadequacy of words unless they're the exact right words. I'm scared of getting their story wrong. I'm scared of letting them down. I gave myself a stern talking-to. If I can't write a decent article at least I can do something practical so I went to the kitchen and bribed the bakers for five loaves of fresh bread. I packed it with some of the food I brought from Paris in the back seat of Hairy Harry's hatchback.

Lejla and Irena were already in the garden with a few students I recognized from the underground café. The sky was smoky but not as much as the day before. It's eerie how scorched air can be so many things. Autumn wildfires and childhood campfires and hundreds of thousands of books in flames. My body felt like it was slowly filling with razor blades. It didn't make sense. All I had to do was ask students what books they needed and why but I was afraid if I opened my mouth – I could feel a scream building inside me.

I hurried into the kitchen and was opening the suitcase when Branka appeared in the doorway. Her Smurfette shirt was spotless. Does her grandma wash it every night? How? There's no water. Branka's English is pretty much limited to "hello" and "I want my MTV" so I made some gestures to ask if she wanted to help. She examined each item as she unpacked it. Parmesan, pickled asparagus, artichokes. It was like she'd never seen food before. The amazement on her face when she took out a tin of butter cookies. I felt sick when she handed it to me and looked away like she couldn't bear the sight of it in case it wasn't real.

There's an outdoor alcove next to the kitchen with a makeshift woodstove on the ground. I managed to get a fire going and opened a few tins of Portuguese sardines and grilled them over the flame. I was so absorbed in keeping the fire going I didn't hear Lejla walk up. Because I was crouched by the stove I had to look up at her. She frowned, and I was positive I was doing something wrong. I waited for her to say something, but it was like she was in a trance. I picked up a piece of bread, spread minced artichoke on it, and topped it with a crisp oily sardine. When I stood up and held it out she stared at me. Branka finally murmured something that must have meant eat. Lejla put the bread in her mouth. I've never seen anyone chew so slowly. Her eyes filled with tears. She spoke softly and I had to lean forward to hear her. She said, "It has not even been six months and already I forgot what it tastes like to be a human being."

<u>8/30, Day 8</u>
<u>11 p.m., Holiday Inn Sarajevo</u>

The next day I bought more bread, and Branka made
a menu and walked around with a pad of paper taking
orders even though everyone gets the same thing.
While the students ate she stood beside them with
her hands behind her back clucking with approval
like an old abuela. It would be adorable if it wasn't so
depressing. When I think of all the flavors I can taste
in Paris just a few hours away. Berthillon's wild straw-
berry sorbet. A little Rochers from the local tabac to
satisfy my sweet tooth. Anything I want. Whenever
I want.

I finally had the chance to talk to Niko. It's dis-
turbing how different this war is for us. The night at
the library shifted something inside me, but for him
it's a run-of-the-mill day in War City. I told him
about Lejla and Irena, and he said it could be a nice
little human interest story if that's what I want to
write. The tone of his voice – I wish it was conde-
scending. That way I could tell him to kiss my grits.
But he was matter of fact. Bobbie was at the piano,
and she kept glancing over at us, so she probably
saw me turn red when Niko said, "Journalism is about
facts, Cub, and human interest stories are about

emotions." He said the problem with emotions is that they can distort facts. I looked around the room. A pile of Dalmatian ham on the buffet while Lejla cried over a sardine. I don't understand. How is that not a plain fact?

<u>9/1, Day 10</u>
<u>6 a.m., Holiday Inn Sarajevo</u>

I wish I could send you my letters, Kate. I wish you could reply and help me make sense of everything. It's hard to picture you and Sven snuggled up reading novels to each other in the wee hours. It's scary how easy it is to forget there's a normal world outside this horror show.

After dinner last night Niko and I stayed in the lobby for drinks. I could tell he knew I was annoyed with him. He didn't like that <u>at all</u>. He was trying to get on my good side, telling a couple journos from Japan how I helped save books at the library and toasting me with plum brandy when Harry Hairy staggered in – another market bombing – bodies everywhere. He said he was shooting the carnage when he saw a little girl wearing a t-shirt with one of those creatures on it. His exact words – "You know the ones, with the blue skin."

It's possible for the world to stop spinning. It's possible for a heart to stop beating. When was the last time I saw Branka? Why would she be at a market? No one takes their children out in the streets anymore. But that's not true because I saw Branka in the street with her grandma that first day I went to the library. I asked Hairy Harry if he was talking about Smurfs. He nodded and said yeah, that's it. That scream I told you about, the one building inside me. It roared in my head. I barely heard my voice crawl out from under it and ask what the girl looked like. Ginger hair, Hairy Harry said. Skin so pale she almost seemed clear.

The earth started spinning again but not fast enough for gravity to get a grip on me. I held on to the table so I wouldn't fly away. The bombs had nothing on my pulse and Hairy Harry said something but I couldn't hear him and I said what, what, what and finally the words crashed through. "She was whimpering, poor poppet, stranded on a pile of rubble and limbs."

She's alive? Hairy Harry nodded. Was she injured? Miraculously no. Everything went a sickly color and Niko must have gotten me upstairs because we were in the room and I was vomiting brandy and I slept and I was awake and then sleeping and then wide awake and I stared at the shadow of Niko snoring beside me and it hit me like a hammer. I followed a total stranger into a war. I flew into a war like it was No Big Deal. War is a Very Big Deal. I felt excruciating pressure like Branka was trying to take shelter inside my rib cage.

I grabbed a notebook and walked out into the hall and around piles of plaster and down to the kitchen to make myself a Nescafé. I had to write my story. Not next week. Not even tomorrow. Now! My nice little FACTUAL human interest story or why was I here? To write Me-Myself-I letters to you and feed people a few lousy sardines? I was so agitated that by the time I noticed Bobbie in one of the lounge chairs in the lobby it was too late to back out. It was like she was waiting for me. She raised a bottle of wine and asked what line Niko used on me – the one about how he'll never run out of work because the world will never run out of war? She said, "I bet he calls you Cub."

There you have it. Me-Myself-I is a cliché on top of everything else. She patted the chair beside her. I sat down. Did I have a choice? She took my coffee out of my hands and gave me a water glass filled with wine. She said, "He never should have brought you here. It was irresponsible." Oh Kate, that's exactly what Kirby said. I remembered my stupid argument with him, telling him how no one's ready for war until they're in one. That's what makes them ready. Guess what? It's not true. So why did I want to keep arguing with Bobbie – protest – tell her I have a journalism degree? I didn't have a chance to say anything because she said, "My friend was shot in the jaw last month. Margaret Moth. Brilliant photojournalist. A true professional." I said I'm sorry but she flapped her hand and sang "invincible, that's what you are" to the tune of the Nat King Cole song. I couldn't tell if she was drunk and I wanted to get away. She looked up and told me in a voice that was very sober, "If you came here because you think you can change the world, think again." My ribs felt like they were going to crack from the pressure. I asked her if she thought she could change the world, and she said, "Not anymore, but history needs witnesses. Bottoms up." I was nauseated but I took a drink. As soon as I did, she said, "If you're going to do this, you can't come unglued every time a market gets bombed."

I told her I know the little girl Hairy Harry was talking about. I told her how Branka pretends she's a waitress and takes people's orders – I was babbling but in my head I knew what I was saying. Tell me what to do, tell me what to do, tell me what to do. I felt this mixture of fear and calm like a storm was coming and I didn't know if it would cleanse me or destroy me.

She said, "In this job you need a place inside your heart that's made of steel." She said you have to be able to live in that place for longer than you'd ever think was bearable. You have to live in there with men who've been tortured in unimaginable ways, and women who've been raped in front of their families, and politicians doing everything wrong or nothing at all because they're calculating their odds of staying in office. She asked me, "Do you have a place like that?"

I flattened my hand over my chest. I felt Branka's feathery trembling. I felt soreness and tenderness in every last soft cell of my heart.

Bobbie asked again. "Do you?" I knew the answer but I didn't want to admit it so I said I'm not sure. "Then you don't," she said, "because if you did, you'd know." It's the truth. I don't have that place in my heart. My face was wet. I felt like a jerk because I wasn't crying for what's happening in Sarajevo. What kind of awful person cries because she's not who she wants to be while sweet little girls like Branka whimper on piles of rubble and human limbs?

I figured Bobbie must think I'm a loser, but she leaned toward me and pulled my head onto her shoulder. She rubbed my back in circles like my mom used to do when I was upset. This made me sob harder. She said, "Sometimes I wish I didn't have steel in my heart. Sometimes I wish someone told me what I'm going to tell you. You can take it or leave it, Cub, but there's no shame in walking away from a war. There is more than one way to make a difference in the world."

9/3, Day 12
In flight to Paris via Zagreb

Dear Kate,

I went back to the house as soon as I could get a ride. Lejla and Irena had moved the tables and typewriters inside. The room was dim because of the plastic over the windows, but there was enough light for me to see how much they'd aged overnight. This was different from after the library bombing. They seemed smaller, thinner, like the war is scraping away the essence of who they are from the inside.

Branka was asleep in a bedroom that was more like a closet in the very back of the house. It's where the family moved her bed when the siege started – although now they sleep at night in a bomb shelter in a basement. There was a dresser with a Smurfette doll on it and a small open window with thin white curtains. A ray of sunlight sliced through the gaps in the fabric. I sat on the floor beside the bed. I needed to hear her breathing. I needed to hear her alive. Most of the thick smoke is gone now, and I smelled crisp traces of autumn on its way, the start of the school year, the shiver of new beginnings. It feels out of place in this city of endless endings. The journos say the London peace conference won't change anything and the mayor says this will be the worst winter Sarajevo has ever seen. Temperatures drop below freezing, and without electricity or oil there won't be any heat. I should have brought bags filled with wool socks. I should have brought suitcases filled with waterproof matches and antibiotics and guns. I don't understand the arms embargo. How can the Bosnians be expected to defend themselves?

I watched a breeze puff the thin curtain in and out. I watched the sheet rise and fall with Branka's steady breathing. I still had <u>Little Women</u> in the bottom of my backpack. I didn't have the chance to return it to the library. I picked up where I left off and started reading out loud, and one by one they joined us. Meg and Jo and Beth and Amy, Marmee and Father, and rowdy Laurie, drowning out the voices of the students in the other room. Muted sunlight moved across the floor. Branka stirred. I climbed onto the bed and she rested her head in my lap while Meg made peace with poverty and Jo walked in the rain with Mr. Bhaer and Amy fell in love with Laurie, and Beth, sweet Beth, why couldn't it be different this time? It seems like it should be the end of the book when she dies, but life keeps going on.

I wasn't done reading, but I suddenly remembered, and I couldn't believe I hadn't looked already. My fingers turned to the last page. There it was. One of Lejla's butterflies. I brushed my fingertip over the purple wings. When she saw my tears, Branka made a small mewing sound like a kitten and petted my arm. At her age I'd never seen an adult cry, but she's seen – I can't breathe when I think about what she's seen. When I think about what's a part of her memories now. If this was Paris or Los Angeles the siege would be over. What makes Sarajevo less valuable to the world? What makes this city's children less valuable? What makes Branka less valuable? The sunlight dissolved up the wall. Branka fell back to sleep. What makes some stories less valuable than others? That's what I can't understand.

PART THREE

And the heart does not die when one thinks it should,

we smile, there is tea and bread on the table.

—Czeslaw Milosz, "Elegy for N.N."

10/17/92

Dear Frida,

I've read your notebook twice. It's like you wrote it in another world. But it's not, which makes everything even harder to comprehend. If you were writing from Mars, I could understand. But you were writing from this very same planet with the very same human beings as the human beings here in Seattle.

You have no idea what a magnificent writer you are, do you? You ~~totally~~ should have told Niko and his "little human interest stories" to kiss your grits. You're writing about people's daily lives like Martha wrote about people's daily lives during wartime in Madrid, and she sure proved there's nothing little about that. You're brave. You're generous. I wish I could hug you right now and tell you something brilliant and comforting, but it's safe to say I'm hardly qualified. Not only am I unbrilliant, I'm a bad person. I'm the only one in the family who lives close enough to see Bumpa during the week as well as on weekends, and sometimes when I'm here I have the most unforgivable thoughts. How much longer do I have to stay? ~~It smells sickly sweet and acrid from the~~

How disgusting am I? Bumpa has to be here twenty-four hours a day, and I complain about afternoon visits.

This has been an extra crummy day. When I got here Bumpa was slouched in his wheelchair by the front window. It shouldn't be such a big deal that one of the nurses parted his hair on the wrong side, but it makes him look like a stranger. We're staring out at gray rain dripping off the fir trees. Actually, I'm the only one staring. He won't open his eyes even though I don't think he's asleep. A nurse yelled in his good ear, "Buck, wake up, you have a visitor!" He blinked a few times and smiled at her. After she left he closed his eyes, and I teased him and said, so you smile for the pretty nurse but not me. He shook his head. I keep telling myself he's not mad at me. He can't walk. He can't feed himself. He's embarrassed. I barely made it to the bathroom before I started bawling.

I'm sorry. I know he's lucky. He has food. He has a safe bed. I know there are more important things in the world. The IRA, Afghanistan, Bosnia. But how are we supposed to get through the day when good men like Bumpa are betrayed by their own bodies and bombs are falling on sweet girls like Branka? How are we supposed to feel all that and function? I only have enough tears for Bumpa. After that, I'm empty. I guess I'm one of those gross selfish twentysomethings who only cares about what happens in my own life.

I mean, look at this letter. You saw brutal things, and I'm whining about this visit. I stopped breathing when I read about snipers shooting at you. I dreamed about it last night. You were in the line of people passing books out of the library, and the books turned into babies. At first when I woke up I thought it was one of those nonsensical things that happens in dreams. But is it? I mean isn't every book its own life? An individual life that lives countless different lives with each different person who reads it. Imagine if every copy of <u>Are You There God</u> in the whole world disappeared? I know it's not scientific proof or anything that different cultures can get along, but look how it shows we have some life in common even though I grew up in small towns and you grew up in a big city and Lejla grew up in a Communist country. Think about all the languages Maya Angelou or J. D. Salinger are translated into. Every book is a conversation we can have around the world. Every book is a conversation we can have with ourselves.

Did you ever feel guilty when you were reading <u>Little Women</u> in Sarajevo? Sometimes I look up from a book and hours have passed, and I haven't thought about Bumpa once. He can't escape his situation. Am I a terrible person for escaping? It's not like I never go back to reality. The second I shut a book, life's right there, front and center. The bees buzzing under my skin. Cement hardening in my throat.

. . . I'm back at my apartment now. I had to stop writing when the nurse brought Bumpa his lunch. Then we watched an <u>I Love Lucy</u> rerun, and he likes "All in a Day's Work" in <u>Reader's Digest</u>, so I read him that. Now it's eight hours later. I got a bug to dig through the boxes in the back of my loft. I was looking for my Judy Blumes, but I ended up taking a trip down memory lane. I found some letters Dad wrote when he traveled on business. He used pictures instead of words so Franny and I had to figure them out like puzzles. And I came across the lobster harmonica Franny bought me the time I got so mad at her for telling me what all my birthday presents were right before I opened them. Why my seven-year-old sister thought that was a good apology, I'll never know, but we still laugh about it.

I didn't find the books I was looking for (Franny probably has them), but it's like my childhood memories were leading me to <u>The House at Pooh Corner</u> instead. I just finished reading it. I'm still crying. When Christopher Robin has to grow up and leave the Hundred Acre Wood, I feel like that's what's happening to me. I'm being shoved out of the woods. I can't do "Nothing" anymore. I have to be a grown-up now. That sounds dumb since a person's twenties are obviously in the grown-up realm, but I don't feel grown-up. It's tattered, but I want you to have my copy.

Love,

Kate

FRIDA RODRIGUEZ ... ~~EN ROUTE~~ *La La Land*

November 12, 1992
Los Angeles, CA

Dear Kate,

Do I feel guilty about disappearing into books? I feel guilty about everything. Hot showers, mascara, my fully intact <u>Tiger Beat</u> collection from 1979, my unbombed bed, chiles rellenos whenever I want them.

I had to get away from Paris. I don't know if I'm going back so write to me here in L.A. for now. My parents still don't know I went to war. When the news is on they shake their heads and tut-tut – how awful – they don't get how twisted it all is. Tom Brokaw telling America about women and children burned alive and then an ad comes on for Wienerschnitzel jalapeño cheese corn dogs. I tried going to a party with some high school friends, and they're more upset about Lenny Kravitz and Lisa Bonet splitting up than the fact that Czechoslovakia is breaking up at this very moment. No one wants to hear about the Serbs and ethnic cleansing. Like no one wanted to hear about the Nazis and their final solution, and look how that ended up. They just crank up Tori Amos and analyze <u>Singles</u> and try to figure out how to find their own Campbell Scott to marry. Talk about gross selfish twentysomethings. Who knows? You're probably right. You're probably one of them too, caring more about Bumpa's stroke than entire cultures ravaged by war. In case you're wondering what kind of disgusting person thinks that about her best friend – me – that's what kind! How's that for truth?

Frida

November 13, 1992
Los Angeles, CA

Dear Kate,

I'M SO SORRY! I shouldn't have mailed that. I was being stupid Me-Myself-I – BLURT! I know it's not an excuse. Ugh – who wants to be their own excuse for bad behavior? You're not gross and selfish. Look at how good you are to Bumpa. You don't always want to be there but you still go. You stay and watch reruns. You don't run away. I ran away from Sarajevo. I ran away from Paris. I'm the biggest jerk in the world. I feel awful. The weather isn't helping. The wind is monstrous! It's thrashing the palm fronds and making a parched rasping sound. I want to crawl out of my skin. PLEASE don't hate me for what I wrote. I didn't mean it. I'm really sorry.

Begging your forgiveness,
Frida

FRIDA RODRIGUEZ ... ~~EN ROUTE~~ La La Land

November 28, 1992
Los Angeles, CA

Dear Kate,

If someone at the store has been complaining about being hung up on, that's me. Frida the Big Chicken – afraid that if you hear my voice you'll be the one who hangs up. Now I've been sitting here for an hour staring at my typewriter. Bock bock bock – that's a Big Chicken sound by the way. Do I tell Kate? Don't I tell Kate? If I tell Kate that will make it real. If I tell her the <u>real</u> reason I went to Sarajevo then she'll know I'm a phony on top of being a selfish jerk.

The Santa Anas are even worse tonight – like someone scraping a razor over my skin. I'm procrastinating. Go on Frida – do it – rip off the Band-Aid. Remember how I told you about my sisters Dolores and Carmen? The Pediatric Surgeon and the Public Defender. Ever since I can remember they told me how important it is to make the world a better place. How important it is as a Chicana woman to pave the way for other Chicana women coming after me so we don't perpetuate toxic cycles. Yes, they talk like that. You think it's hard for people like us now? They started out in the 1960s. They made sure I didn't do drugs or "fall in with any hoodlums" – they also talk like <u>that</u> – and when they saw how much I love writing they decided I'd be the first Mexican-American woman to win a Pulitzer Prize in journalism. I didn't have any better ideas so why not?

After I graduated from college I jumped from job to job until a professor hooked me up with the finance paper. It was no-brainer work because the clients basically wrote the articles for us and the money was great and by the time I'd been doing it a year I had a Jetta and my own apartment in Beachwood Canyon. Then one day my sisters took me out to lunch – Spago – that's how I knew something was up. $12 duck sausage pizza is for special occasions in our family, not lunch on any old Tuesday. I'm thinking someone's sick in a way you don't recover from. I can barely hold down my chopped salad when Dolores gives Carmen a side look and Carmen puts down her fork and says, "You can do better, Frida." I was sitting there head to toe in Esprit with a Capezio purse and an L.L.Bean bomber jacket hanging off my chair. My Mariah Carey perm cost $65. Dolores and Carmen helped take care of me when Mom traveled for work. They know how much I look up to them. It was a real gut punch. Carmen's tone of voice said what she really meant. We're disappointed in you.

What was I supposed to say? I'm not like them. I barely managed to graduate with a B average from college. I genuinely tried to master the inverted pyramid but you know me. Structure isn't my strong suit. After my sisters confronted me, I thought if I backed myself into a corner, some kind of journalism magic would happen. My inner Edward R. Murrow would kick in, and

I'd make them proud of me. I was bluffing and Sarajevo called my bluff. And you know what I discovered? If I'm mediocre at something I don't care about – no harm, no foul. But if I care – I had no idea how much I was going to care about Sarajevo, Kate. I get what you mean about being drop-kicked out of the Hundred Acre Wood. After Sarajevo I can never go back to my innocence.

I'm going to call my old boss at <u>West Coast Commerce</u> and ask for my McJob back. I'll ditch my antiquated typewriter and get myself one of those new Macintosh PowerBooks and discuss <u>Mad About You</u> around the water cooler. If I can't make the world better, at least I'll have moolah so I can donate to the kind of people I'm not so they can make a difference.

Yours in failure,

Frida

Fair Kate's Friends Forever Mixtape for Frida

1. True Colors – Cyndi Lauper

2. Thank You for Being a Friend – <u>Golden Girls</u> version

3. That's What Friends Are For – Dionne Warwick version

4. We Go Together – <u>Grease</u>

5. With a Little Help from My Friends – Beatles version

6. With a Little Help from My Friends – Joe Cocker version
   (I couldn't decide)

7. You've Got a Friend – Carole King

8. Lean on Me – Fair Kate the Bookseller version

THE PUGET SOUND BOOK COMPANY

101 South Main Street   Seattle, WA 98104

12/7/92

Dear Frida,

I hope you like the mixtape. It's been a while since I've made one. I'm pretty sure the last one was for a high school boyfriend. I'm having flashbacks about trying to record Journey and Loverboy off the radio. I also hope you get the point of it, FRIEND!

News Flash: Trying something that doesn't work out doesn't make you a phony. You get on my case to stop talking about what I don't know. Well, you need to stop looking at what you didn't do and look at what you did. It was exactly what your sisters wanted. When you grilled those sardines, you made the world a better place. You showed Lejla, Irena, and the other students that someone cares about them. Maybe it wasn't a Pulitzer Prize–winning article, but it mattered to them that you cared. You still care. Don't go back to <u>West Coast Commerce</u>.

For the record, I'm Fair Kate, not Fairweather Kate. I wasn't mad at you, even though that was pretty rude. Apology accepted. (On that note, you might want to lighten up on your friends. I liked <u>Singles</u>, too. They filmed a lot of it around the bookstore which was pretty cool.) The reason I didn't respond right away is because things haven't been going great. It's not just Bumpa. Ever since his stroke, something's been off-kilter between Sven and me. I tried writing to you about it a couple times. Usually when I do that things start to clear up, but lately I feel like everything's getting muddier, especially after this morning.

Sven's been in a super low mood because he's had a few rejections for his novel. Last night at a party he and this famous British novelist got into a gripe-fest about the commodification of the publishing industry. The writer's wife belted back one too many, and she pulled me aside and whispered, "Consider yourself warned. Here's the thing about a great writer. His ambition will make him bitter." On the drive home, Sven went on a jag about how most people plod along not caring if they do anything meaningful with their lives, but he's trying with his novel and no one appreciates it.

When I met Mom at the nursing home today, the night was stuck in my head like clumps of wet cotton. We were in the game room working on a jigsaw puzzle. She'd find a piece and then give it to Bumpa. His good hand is pretty shaky, so he'd get a piece close to where it was supposed to go, and she'd wrap her hand around his and they'd press it in together. One piece after another. Every once in a while she asked him if he was warm enough or if he'd rather watch TV like everything was normal. Like it's perfectly acceptable to be a good person and love your family and work all your life and take your car in for an oil change every three months until the scumbag universe decides to reciprocate by knocking you flat with a stroke.

~~What's the point in~~ I started to feel tight like I did that day in Toppenish. Frida, I'm so tired of Big Questions barging into my head. I could feel this one swelling inside me, and when Bumpa fell asleep, I couldn't hold it back. I had to know if Mom thought Bumpa had a happy life.

The second I asked, I knew what I wanted her to say. Please say yes. Please say it was real happiness and please tell me how you know. She reached out and brushed a strand of his thin gray hair away from his forehead, gently like you do with a child so you don't wake them up. She was quiet for a while and then she whispered, "Chicago was hard, but I think he made peace with it."

Chicago? Peace with what? It turns out that not long after I was born, Bumpa disappeared from Seattle. No one knew where he went until he called his sister and told her he was working at a factory in Chicago. I asked Mom why I never heard this story, and she said it was all such a long time ago. He came back a few months later, went to a psychiatrist for his depression, and got better. Bumpa was depressed, Frida. Gentle, smiling Bumpa who spent hours teaching Franny and me how to carve soap and build ships in bottles went to a psychiatrist! What happened? Was he questioning who he was? Did he figure it out? More questions ping-ponged in my head, but Mom's lips were tight the way they get when she's trying not to cry. She slid her hand across the table and softly touched her fingertips to Bumpa's fingertips. My anxiety hit me so hard my earlobes tingled.

When I got to the store, Sven was downstairs setting up for the Cynthia Kadohata reading. I told him what Mom told me.

He nodded like he wasn't surprised and asked if I've read <u>Walden</u>. Then he quoted how the mass of men lead lives of quiet desperation. Seriously? I share that Bumpa was so depressed he fled all the way across the country, and that's the best I get? Fortune cookie Thoreau?

Writing to you may not be solving anything, but it sure makes me feel better to let it out (to you, not just anybody, but YOU). Your faithful BEST FRIEND forever,
Kate

FRIDA RODRIGUEZ ... ~~EN ROUTE~~ *La La Land*

December 13, 1992
Los Angeles, CA

Dear Kate,

   I love the mixtape – you can lean on me too – and I need to make something right. When I read your letter about Bumpa's stroke, the very first thing I should have written to you is how sorry I am. That was inexcusable. I am so sorry, Kate. It's not fair and it stinks and I know that's not eloquent like Sven but it's from my heart. Now I'm going to call the store and not hang up and tell you how truly sorry I am.

Love,

Frida

FRIDA RODRIGUEZ ... ~~EN ROUTE~~ La La Land

January 18, 1993
Los Angeles, CA

Fair Kate,

It feels weird – good weird – writing to you again after a month of phone calls. I've got your mixtape playing in the background. I still laugh every time you sing "Lean on Me." Do not quit your day job to try out for <u>Star Search</u>!

I could tell you what I'm about to write over the phone, but I want to put this on paper for posterity. I'm going back to France! You're never going to believe it, but Lejla showed up at La Louisiane looking for me. Somehow she ran into Kirby and he gave her my address in L.A. She wrote and said it's getting worse in Bosnia than anything we see on the news, which doesn't seem possible since the news is sickening. She brought lists of books the students need, and she's working with organizations like the Helsinki Citizens' Assembly that's setting up sites for donated materials around Europe. Reading her letter, I felt detestable. I should have been in Paris when she arrived. I should have been reaching out to college newspapers around the U.S. like I talked about with her and Irena to raise awareness for their project. And who is going to help her get books into Sarajevo? They can't just be mailed. I have contacts now. Niko! Harry Hairy! Bobbie! Every time a journalist comes out and goes back in, they can do it – book by book. Why not?

Speaking of Kirby. Confession: I didn't tell you this before because I wasn't sure how he'd respond, but I wrote him a letter telling him he was right and I'm really sorry for being such a stubborn jerk. You know what he replied? "Who cares who's right? I'm just glad you're safe." Talk about making me feel even worse – but better too. I can't imagine being back in Paris without him. A Pop Rocks personality like me needs a stable Kirby in her life.

I'm terrified I'm going to blow my big comeback so whenever you see me doing something stupid – BIG stupid, not my usual daily stupid – kick me in the seat of the pants and set me straight. Imperfectly yours,
Frida

P.S. I'll be in Paris in two weeks so send your reply to the hotel.

2/4/93

Dear Frida,

I'm so, so, so, so overjoyed that you're back in Paris. And that you made up with Kirby. It's about time! I'll miss our calls, but you're meant to do things that matter. And if we're making things official, I'm doubling down on my argument in our last call. Serving those sardines in Sarajevo mattered! I also want it on the record how much I appreciate you letting me hog our conversations talking about Bumpa and Sven. Thank goodness our phone bills weren't prorated or I'd be flat broke and not just regular broke.

I'm in a decent mood. It's strange how my anxiety comes in waves. I'm not sure what makes the waves wash in and out, but it's nice when they're out. It's nice when something good happens with Bumpa, and my brain doesn't torture me with questions about happiness and unexamined lives and what made him go to Chicago. Like the last time I was with him, I was fiddling around with a deck of cards playing War. I had to take the turns for both of us. At least I thought I did. I was kind of drifting in and out of my thoughts when I realized his good hand was crawling across the table toward the two cards I'd turned up. A three for me and a king for him. He pulled the cards toward himself. I know his brain works, but it's easy to forget because he can't speak. I turned over two more cards. I think I was holding my breath. He blinked at them and pushed them toward me. I kept going. He took the pair if he won or pushed them over to me if I won. We ended up playing War all afternoon. I could hardly believe it, Frida. It was like we were us again. Bumpa and Punkin playing cards together like we used to. Now I'm crying.

. . . I'm back. Roy gave me one of his Roy hugs. He's surprisingly sturdy for such a slender guy. Then Stella sent me to the coatroom for a good weep. It turns out her whole rebel thing is a facade. I'm pretty sure she has a crush on Birkenstock-wearing Otis. He's a softy who's always going on about social issues in Latin America and trying to get everyone to read I, Rigoberta Menchú. Stella is really smart (Frida Rodriguez smart). We've had some pretty deep conversations about Robertson Davies and

. . . You're never going to believe this. We just caught spies. Kids Books Josephine was cleaning out the little castle we have for kids to play in, and she looked out the turret and saw two people taking photos and measuring shelves. We're 99% sure they're from Forth & Regal. They're opening a superstore in Bellevue in May, and they're planning one somewhere in Seattle after that. Don't they know bookstores aren't Kmarts. Seattle might put up with a few generic chains like B. Dalton or Waldenbooks, but no way is it going to support a corporate behemoth. Hand-Selling Forever!! (This month it's A Circle of Quiet, by the way.)

I've completely lost track of where I was going. Oh yeah. I want to tell you that I took your Ma Bell advice and invited Sven to the nursing home with me, but the day we planned to go, he got the tenth (gulp) rejection for his novel. He was too morose to take anywhere. Editors say the writing is exceptional but the story is too dense. I feel bad for him, especially since I had a thought about what his agent said. About how Sven could be the next John Updike. That seemed like a positive thing at the time, but now I wonder, what if the world doesn't want a next Updike? Sure he won the Pulitzer, but look at what's hot. <u>Clockers</u> and <u>The Mysteries of Pittsburgh</u>. Did I ever tell you the title of Sven's novel? <u>Into the Liminal Gloaming</u>. I had to look up both words in my <u>American Heritage</u>. The writing really is exceptional, but between you and me, I don't think it should take forty-six pages for a husband and wife to drive up a hill.

Love,

Kate

FRIDA RODRIGUEZ ... EN ROUTE *Again!*

March 19, 1993
Paris, France

Fair Kate,

Sorry it took so long to write back. I hit the ground running as soon as I got here, and when I picked up your letter again last night, I couldn't believe how much time had passed.

Hopefully Sven's had a greedy bite on his novel by now, but if he hasn't, you might be right. No one is meant to be the next Updike because even if this Brave New World wasn't obsessed with reading books like <u>Generation X</u>, no one is meant to be the next anyone else. Like me. I'm not meant to be the next Dolores or Carmen – how does enlightenment look on me?

About that game of War with Bumpa. You guys used to spend hours playing cards together so when you think about it, it's not <u>like</u> you're "us again" – you <u>are</u> "us again" – just in a different smelly setting.

Backtracking! Right before I left L.A. I fessed up to Sarajevo. I wasn't planning to but Mom made a going-away dinner – chiles rellenos naturally – and my sisters came over. I'm telling everyone about this incredible tagine I had on the Left Bank and Mom's interrogating me about the ingredients because she's never met a recipe she doesn't want to try. Right in the middle of explaining the pickled lemons I broke open like a cracked dam. Not about the snipers at the library – I didn't want to completely freak them out – but a lot of it because I realized I wanted them to know why I had to go back to Paris.

Dad got very, very quiet. It was impossible to tell what Carmen and Dolores were thinking, which was unsettling because usually when they think it – they say it! Then Mom said, "Oh Frida, this is why I worry about you. You have such a tender heart." Can you believe it? Echoes of Bobbie. Things got strained – not a typical Rodriguez dinner table free-for-all and I was sure they were upset with me – not to mention disappointed – what a cruddy way to leave but when I got back to Paris and unpacked I found a package hidden in my suitcase. A cassette of <u>Les Misérables</u> – Dad and I went four times when it came to the Schubert – and a Ziploc of Mom's homemade tortillas.

My first night back I fired up my hot plate and warmed up those gorgeous corn crêpes smeared with creamy French butter and listened to "I Dreamed a Dream" until the sun came up. "Then I was young and unafraid and dreams were made and used and wasted." Isn't that a hard truth! And the tortillas. Some food tastes exactly like home. It got me thinking about Sarajevo and how if people there can't have the food they grew up with do they feel homeless even though they're still living in their homes?

It feels strange to be here. Mostly because it doesn't feel strange. The hotel gave me my old room back, and Kirby helped me arrange it like it was before I left except nicer because Lejla bought postcards of Degas' Cambodian dancers and stuck them on the wall. Yesterday he took me to Barthélemy for a goat cheese that tasted like burnt toast and it was nice to be back in our old rhythm, debating every little thing that crossed our minds. Then when we were walking back to the hotel, he offered to help with – get ready for it, Fair Kate – Branka!

Irena's sister – Branka's mom in case you forgot – won't leave Sarajevo because obviously surgeons are needed now more than ever, and their grandma refuses to leave. They wanted Branka out of the country, and Irena didn't want to leave their grandma alone plus who would manage the project once books started coming in? So Branka came with Lejla to Paris. They're staying with some people who help refugees but Lejla doesn't like leaving Branka with strangers while she works. Now Branka is curled up in my bed while I type this letter to you! She can sleep through mortars so of course she can sleep through typing. How sad is that?

Love,

Frida

P.S. I keep forgetting to ask. What's a stripped mass market?

P.S. Deux. Confession: Remember when I told you about my haircut? The only reason À bout de souffle is my favorite French New Wave movie is because it's the only one I've seen that didn't put me to sleep. Have you ever watched one? There's a reason for the phrase "watching paint dry." Confession Deux: I loved Ghost. Confession Trois while I'm at it: When I described my Julie

Christie sweater in my first letter to the bookstore I was really thinking about Andie MacDowell's long cable knit sweater in <u>St. Elmo's Fire</u>, but I wanted whoever opened it to think I was worldly.

P.S. Trois. Guess what came in the mail today right before I sealed this envelope? A big fat Xerox of listings of all the university newspapers in America. From my sisters! How's that for a vote of confidence? I've written a standard pitch to explain Lejla and Irena's project, and then I tailor each letter to the university I'm sending it to. "Since Berkeley has such a long history of student activism, I think there will be interest in . . ." Or "Given Carleton College's apartheid boycotts and successful divestment from South Africa . . ." Researching each school and making sure each pitch sounds personal is taking up all my spare time – but I promise my next reply won't take so long.

3/30/93

Dear Frida,

Lejla is so lucky to have you in her life. And <u>West Coast Commerce</u>'s loss is the world's gain. But you haven't mentioned writing since you left Sarajevo. I noticed it during our phone calls when you were in L.A. Maybe I should have said something then. You are going to keep writing, aren't you? The only answer I will accept is yes. I figured maybe you need a little prod, so I went to the galley box (that's where our book buyer puts prepublication copies that all the different publishers send us). I told it, "Give me a book for Frida." I closed my eyes and reached in, and I swear this is true. I pulled out <u>The Balkan Express</u>. The interesting thing about Slavenka Drakulić is that her Me-Myself-I writing doesn't feel self-centered. It makes me feel like I'm experiencing what she experienced right along with her. You should stop resisting your amazing Frida-ness. "Pick up where the news stops," like Slavenka says. (There's a line near the beginning of the book that especially made me think of you. I want to see if you find it on your own.)

I wish I could say I've been writing too, but mostly I've been avoiding it by cooking. Today I'm perfecting Laurie Colwin's tomato pie recipe (the biscuit-dough crust is tricky), even though every time I drizzle the lemon and mayo I start crying. I still can't believe she died. She was only forty-eight. I was just getting to know her. I remember when I was reading <u>Home Cooking</u>, I'd have these daydreams about how she'd write more books and I'd read them, and one day I'd meet her and gush about how much she means to me. She introduced me to polenta and olive oil. She took away my fear of eggplant with its prehistoric starfish stem and vinyl skin. She burned food and sometimes drank too much wine and didn't seem to agonize at all over who she was supposed to be. She didn't write a so-called Big Important Novel, but when I read <u>Happy All the Time</u> ~~it made me feel The way the character Holly serves tea in her unmatched I want to decant things in glass~~ Give me a second to nail down this thought. Five minutes. Ten minutes. Got it (sort of).

~~When I'm feeling blue and redo my address book with colored pens to cheer myself up, Laurie makes me feel like I'm not devising~~ Ugh. Why can't I figure out what I want to say? Laurie's characters think a lot about the way life works, but they let themselves really enjoy it, too, and I guess the way they live got me thinking more about Sven's whole constructed happiness theory. I'm not sure I agree with it. Like the other day when I was especially sad about Bumpa, I hopped in Edith Wharton (that's what I named my car) and drove down to Sears. It has a big craft section, and I wanted to buy rope so Bumpa and I could do macrame.

He loves tying knots. I think it's a sailor thing. When we're working on macrame together I'm happy, and I can tell he's happy, too. It doesn't feel artificial at all, and it makes me wonder if Sven's right, or if there's a reason he needs to think some kinds of happiness are real and some aren't.

I tried asking him, but he didn't want to talk about it. He's in such a funk about his novel. Confession: I didn't mind since I've pretty much stopped talking to him about Bumpa anyway. It's like I live two totally different lives. Like last weekend I spent Saturday at the nursing home and Sunday with Sven. We took the ferry to Bainbridge Island and drove around looking at old-fashioned farmhouses, figuring out how much money we'd need to live there and write books and raise a family. When we went down to the beach overlooking the city, we wrapped up in a blanket, and we could see the skyline from the Space Needle all the way down to Mount Rainier. We talked for hours like when we first got together. He really opened up to me in a new way.

I knew diabetes can affect a person's eyes, but I didn't know he went to the doctor recently because he's had some black spots in his vision. His voice sounded frail when he told me how afraid he is of losing his eyesight. There's this quote he read by Oliver Wendell Holmes. It's about how so many people die with their music still inside them. Sven's terrified of going blind before he publishes his novel. He says he doesn't mean to be so bleak all the time. He wants to have more picnics in department stores and dance in more heat waves, but he's afraid of running out of time. There's already so much darkness in the world, Frida. What if the dark spots on his soul keep growing like the ones in his vision? It scares me. He says he's thankful for the light I bring into his life, but what if I don't have enough light for both of us?

I've been thinking about what Bobbie said about a steel place in a person's heart. I'm pretty sure I don't have one either, and I wonder if some people have a place that's extra tender. Everything makes me cry these days. The poor people on that ferry in Haiti. The World Trade Center bombing. Laurie Colwin, Bumpa, Sven's eyesight. That stupid Fruit of the Loom ad with the song about teaching your children well. It's like all the compartments in my heart collapsed and I feel everything all at once.

Love,

Kate

P.S. I guessed at Branka's size for the Smurfette dress, and I hope she likes <u>Ramona the Pest</u>. I thought you could use it to help teach her English. If she doesn't like it I can send something different like <u>Frog and Toad</u>.

P.P.S. If a book doesn't sell we can return it to the publisher and get a refund. Because mass market paperbacks are so cheap, it's more expensive to mail the whole book back than it's worth, so we strip off the covers, throw the books away, and send the covers back to the publisher to get our money back. That's a stripped mass market.

FRIDA RODRIGUEZ ... EN ROUTE

April 14, 1993
Paris, France

Fair Kate,

I get what you're saying about darkness. I'm scared of it too. You're right. It's everywhere. I'm sick of round-the-clock satellite news. And did you ever see those devastating Benetton ads? I hate having such a tender heart. There's this look that crosses Lejla's face – wondering if her family and very best friend in the whole world are still alive. But somehow she moves forward. If she can do it we can too. You won't want to hear this, but if you can't let your lives with Sven and Bumpa come together, you're going to have a hard time moving forward with the rest of your life.

When I told the translation company what I'm doing, they helped me extend my visa, and they let me work from the hotel so I can watch Branka while Lejla runs around the city. After she's done she comes over and we go through the responses I've been getting from universities. Then I read <u>Ramona</u> to Branka. She's absorbing English like a sponge. She adores Ramona Quimby. Sometimes an image pops into my head. The one from Hairy Harry of Branka standing in the bombed market. I think – Go

Ramona go! Push that ugliness out of her head. Give her new memories so twenty years from now when she thinks about being six she remembers naughty Ramona hiding behind the garbage cans with Ribsy. Or at least she has options to choose from.

Please send the rest of the Ramona books and another book like Slavenka. What a difference from Martha. Her presence is such an important part of the stories she's telling. I'm trying to figure out how she does it without making it about her. Is this the line you were talking about? "I ended up writing a book because, in spite of everything, I still believe in the power of words." I wish I could keep believing that but it's hard when I think about the library burning.

Sometimes it feels like it didn't happen at all, but then other times, like when I hear a siren or a loud crash, I flinch. And I keep having dreams that I'm in the bathtub trying to scrub smoke out of my hair. I was only there for two weeks, and it changed my life, but Confession Fair Kate: I'm not sure I should write anymore. We know now I'm not a War Journo Dame and it's not like I'm doing anything interesting like Slavenka. I write letters to college newspapers to get the word out about the books we need and otherwise try to make things better for Lejla. Like the other day I went to the Yugoslavian embassy and asked the receptionist what I can make for a friend who's homesick. She said bosanski lonac is one of the country's traditional dishes. There are different ways to make it depending on the region and even the family but the base ingredients are usually the same. Big chunks of meat with cabbage, peppers, potatoes, tomatoes, carrots, onions, and garlic. I got fresh parsley and whole black peppercorns from a regular market but I had to hike all over the city to track down a seasoning called Vegeta.

Branka and I cooked all day. I let her pick out a sunny yellow cloth at Le Bon Marché and we draped it over my desk. I invited Kirby, and he brought a baguette and Beaujolais. When Lejla arrived she froze in the doorway. Her nostrils flared. When she saw the Vegeta beside the stew simmering on my hot plate – her expression softened for the first time since I've seen her in Paris. Branka danced from foot to foot she was so excited. Lejla dipped a spoon into the pot and took a bite. She chewed the meat. I thought about how I feel when I eat chiles rellenos. That's how I wanted her to feel. I was ridiculously nervous. I was sure I blew it somehow and she was trying to figure out how to be polite.

Her eyes grew wet and she said, "You must think something is wrong with me, I cry every time you give me food." The more I get to know Lejla, the more I understand how much her raccoon eyeliner is a disguise like your friend Stella's grunge chick look. Whenever she comes over she brings a thoughtful gift. Last night's was an old-fashioned teacup she turned into a little pot for African violets, and you know what – it made me happy. And even if it was Old Sven's artificially constructed happiness, who cares? It felt good.

While we ate Kirby asked Lejla about the library and they sounded like professors, analyzing how extreme changes in a city's physical environment cause extreme changes in a community. Kirby says architecture is directly related to a sense of identity. It's not just that the library's design recognized Bosnia's Muslim population. It's also about the building being there over time. People walk past it and it anchors their sense of place and their feelings of security about who they are in that place. He explained how buildings are a way for people to communicate across generations, and I felt like he really understood what happened – not just intellectually but emotionally – when he said destroying a building like the library destroys messages across time.

Branka conked out, and I nodded off, but Kirby and Lejla talked until three a.m. Remember when you wrote about dinner with Coleslaw Meatloaf? That's how I felt while they were talking. Minus the Neil Diamond. They're so sure of what they're supposed to do in the world. What if I'm one of those people who never figures that out?

Love from your friend who's way too old to still be this uncertain about life,

Frida

P.S. Did you notice there are only six dashes in this whole letter? I'm working hard on getting them out of my repertoire.

P.S. Deux. You might have to send another Smurf dress because Branka won't take it off. She even sleeps in it. I had to bribe her with pain au chocolat the other day so I could wash it.

4/29/93

Dear Frida,

It's a perfect spring day. Before work Stella and I bought cinnamon rolls at Grand Central Bakery across the street. Then we walked around to Torrefazione for coffee. We sat in the cobblestone square, and it was like being in a European village where you know everyone. Birkenstock Otis was playing hacky sack with a couple guys from the store, and the barista kept asking if we needed anything because he has the hots for Stella. A few tables over, David Ishii was reading the paper. He has a used bookshop near ours. Most of his stock is about baseball and fly-fishing. The sunlight felt like a warm bath, and even though it's almost nine now, we have the front door propped open. I can smell creosote and soft salt air off the water even back here at the information desk.

I know what you mean about those Benetton ads. They hit me hard, especially the one with the man dying of AIDS. The first time I saw it, it made me think about how there are so many things in this world I can't fix, and when I start thinking how it's possible for CNN to never run out of misery to report on twenty-four hours a day, it feels like I'm made of thousands of live electrical currents. Is it gross to say I miss not knowing so much? I remember when life was half an hour of Walter Cronkite, then homework, Happy Days and Laverne & Shirley, and if you fell asleep on the couch you woke up to a test pattern with colored stripes on the screen, not more bad news. Do you think it's possible for kids these days to feel as innocent as we used to feel?

I've never thought about buildings the way Kirby does, so I decided to test his ideas and walk to the store from Pike Place Market along the waterfront. Highway 99 roared above me, and out on the water the ferries trailed bubbling white wakes. It turns out almost every building I passed holds memories of Bumpa. Whenever we made trips into Seattle, we'd have fried clam strips at Ivar's. He'd buy Franny and me paper cocktail umbrellas for our Barbies at Trident Imports, and we'd stop at Ye Olde Curiosity Shop and say hello to Sylvester, this dried-up mummy someone found in the Arizona desert. I was standing there looking at Sylvester, and all of a sudden Bumpa chuckled and said, "Golly, that geezer sure had a bum day." I didn't imagine the words in my head, Frida. Bumpa was there, and I realized he'll always be there as long as the building is there. But what if it's torn down? Obviously that memory is inside me, but would I ever hear that chuckle again without Ye Olde Curiosity Shop to jog it loose? It makes me think about Sven's blind spots. What if every familiar place that disappears from your life leaves a shadow in your memory? Is there such a thing as memory blindness? How

KIM FAY

can the people in Sarajevo remember who they were if there's nothing left to remind them?

I should probably explain all the goodies I'm sending along with the rest of the Ramona series. I hit the jackpot with a Yugoslavian cookbook at Half Price Books in the U District. Stella and I drive up there in her Karmann Ghia (much cooler than my Chevette) and cruise the shelves. We like Twice Sold Tales on Capitol Hill, too, because we can have coffee and crème brûlée afterward at B&O Espresso. I found a first edition of <u>Moon Tiger</u> the other day (I'm keeping that one for me). For your woman like Slavenka, I choose <u>The Road Through Miyama</u>. Leila Philip went to Japan to apprentice with a potter. She weaves a tapestry out of history, culture, and her own experiences, like harvesting rice.

I'm also sending <u>The English Patient</u>. The writing is so gorgeous I can't stand it. Not Sven-liminal-gloaming gorgeous but gorgeous like perfect poetry that doesn't make you scratch your head and feel two inches tall. That's not why I picked it, though. I think it shows how many different ways there are to write about war. You just have to find yours. Actually, I know yours, but I'm not saying because you'll say No Way, Fair Kate. Never mind. I am saying it. Your way is by writing about food. Trust me. Your descriptions of cooking for Lejla and her response when she tastes the bosanski lonac are so moving.

One more thing. Don't EVER say you're going to stop writing again. I forbid it! In fact, I demand that you write something about your experiences and send it to me with your next letter. An

essay. A want ad. A to-do list. If you don't, you'll force me to make another mixtape starting with "Eye of the Tiger."
Love from your friend who's as old as you and still
uncertain, too,
Kate

P.S. I'm okay with you ditching dashes, but I miss your marathon run-on sentences.

Leaving for the night, my friend Lejla turned in the doorway of my hotel room and looked at me, her eyebrows angled with serious thought. Her white T-shirt shouted bold black advice: FRANKIE SAY RELAX. She glanced at six-year-old Branka sleeping on my bed in her Smurfette dress. She had a full day coming up so Branka would stay the night with me.

"Is everything okay?" I asked. Her expression made me apprehensive. There are stretches of time when I forget about being in the war, and there are suddenly moments like this when I know Sarajevo is always with me. An uninvited dinner guest blending into the wallpaper until suddenly piping up to mention he poisoned the soup. I lowered my voice. "Is Irena okay?"

"Irena?" Lejla's voice tripped on the name of her best friend still in Bosnia. "She is fine. Will you make bosanski lonac again on Sunday?"

Of course.

"Will you make double the amount?"

She liked it, she really liked it! Bien sûr!

"My mother uses more fresh parsley on top," she informed me gruffly. She held out her hand palm down and rubbed her thumb back and forth over her fingertips. "How do you say?"

"Sprinkled?"

"Sprinkled." She repeated the word a few times. "Do not be so stingy with the paprika."

People who have opinions are the best kind.

On Sunday I borrowed an extra hot plate from the Nigerian sculptor down the hall. I arranged it with mine on a small folding table I bought at Les Puces flea market along with a proper knife, an enormous stockpot, a giant frying pan, and a cutting board that covers my desk. The board had to be strapped to the roof of Kirby's miniature Citroën along with the table. Voilà! La petite kitchen.

Along with bosanski lonac, I decided to make ćevapi, a sausage recipe from a Balkan cookbook sent to me by a brilliant bookseller in America. Don't be stingy with the paprika? Mission accomplished! While the bosanski lonac simmered, I massaged baking soda and cold water into the ground beef to tenderize the mixture. I'd returned to the Yugoslavian embassy to ask for advice, and the receptionist told me this technique is what gives the little sausages their smooth texture. That and having the butcher grind the meat twice.

"If there is any left . . ." The receptionist said this shyly as I was leaving.

I bought containers to take leftovers to this apple-cheeked woman, and for Lejla since I assumed that was why she wanted me to double the bosanski lonac. But she had something else in mind. When she arrived, she wasn't alone.

"This is Merjema. She is a Muslim refugee." Lejla frowned,

adding, "As you know it is not the same as being a Christian refugee in Western Europe."

On CNN Muslim women in burkas are the subjugated wives of terrorists. In the Hôtel La Louisiane, economics major Merjema wore a string tie with an Oxford shirt, stone-washed jeans, and high-tops.

I sent Branka downstairs to the hotel kitchen to borrow an extra bowl. We spread the sunflower-yellow tablecloth on the floor. My heart pounded. Lejla is my friend, and I'm sure that's why she liked the bosanski lonac so much. No matter how bad food is, we taste it with generosity if it's made for us by a friend with a tender heart.

Merjema didn't know me. Her judgment would be objective.

Branka set out the dishes as if we had dinner with friends on the floor every night. She begged to light the honeysuckle candle that Lejla had brought. Her pale eyes grew wide as she used the match to ignite the wick. Despite being a child of war, she's still young enough for innocent pleasures. A shiny striped snail in the garden at the Musée Rodin. A cup of cocoa at Christian Constant. A dancing candle flame.

I set out store-bought flatbread to eat with the sausages along with raw onion slices and a jar of ajvar, a thick sauce of roasted red peppers and eggplant that I got from Apple Cheeks at the embassy. Lejla was right about more paprika in the bosanski lonac. It lured the essence of the beef to the surface where it bounced enthusiastically off the freshness of the parsley.

The ćevapi was already off to a rough start since I didn't have a grill and had to pull a MacGyver with the frying pan. And I should have used a mixture of beef and lamb or beef and pork, but I wasn't sure if Lejla eats pork, and I can't bring myself to serve Mary's little lamb on a dinner table. The problem with using only one kind of meat is the risk of dryness, but the baking soda seemed to do the trick. I worried I'd traveled too South of the Border on the cayenne. Mom's chorizo makes my mouth euphoric with stinging pain, but I don't think that's the goal of Yugoslavian cuisine.

As we ate, the silence around our indoor picnic grew. The night was stuffy with unseasonal spring heat. The open windows called in vain for a breeze. Did Merjema like the meal? Did she hate it? Branka ate like usual, snuffling happily like a little piglet. She doesn't count because her favorite meal is the canned sloppy joe Kirby buys her at The General Store on rue de Grenelle. Merjema ate slowly. Lejla had a funny grin on her face. Was she embarrassed for me?

World peace didn't depend on this meal. Why did I feel like it did?

As I refilled Merjema's glass of iced tea, she said, "When Lejla told me an American made bosanski lonac almost as good as her mother's, I did not believe her." She smiled. "I believe her."

Her praise was the breeze I'd been waiting for. It whisked into the room, and conversation unfurled like a flag catching a current of air. We talked about the food and they told me how in Bosnia it's considered important to "eat something with a spoon every day" because it's healthy. And apparently ćevapi is rarely eaten at home for a regular meal. It's more like a barbecue food. Plus it's too heavy. Then Lejla explained how she's never seen ajvar in a ćevap restaurant. Ćevapi is usually served with raw onions and a scoop of kajmak, which is a kind of clotted cream, and ajvar is served with regular bread or on an appetizer tray. I thought about how complex Mexican food is and felt a little thrill at how much there is to learn about Bosnian cuisine.

After a while Lejla told Merjema how I helped rescue books from the burning library, and Merjema told us her father is an Islamic scholar. When she was young he took her to the library and showed her ancient Arabic manuscripts. She said the jeweled colors of the illuminated pages were so enticing her father would laugh and threaten to tie her hands behind her back with her hair ribbon so she wouldn't touch them. Filling another piece of flatbread with ćevapi, she said softly, "I wish I had touched them." As if this could have changed their fate.

When I set out a bowl of bright, jammy strawberries, Lejla clapped her hands and murmured, "When I was little strawberries meant summer was on the way."

"We spent holidays on the Adriatic," Merjema said, her full lips shining with red juice.

"My family has a cottage near Dubrovnik on the sea," Lejla told her, and then murmured sadly, "I wonder what has happened to it." They talked about their childhoods, slipping in and out of English until they left me altogether. I couldn't understand their words, but I understood they had found a way back home.

I eased away from the tablecloth. I put a finger to my lips, shh, and beckoned Branka to the bed. We made a nest of pillows, and

I read to her, keeping my voice low. Being quiet became a game, and whenever Ramona did something funny, instead of laughing, Branka's warm body shivered against mine.

The room grew dark. I turned on the small bedside lamp. On the wall, Degas' Cambodian dancers seemed to sway in the dusk. I read until Branka grew heavy at my side. I closed the book and looked up. How long had Lejla and Merjema been listening to me?

"You will keep reading?" Lejla whispered.

I kept reading.

About Beezus and Ramona to two dark-haired refugees living in a foreign country a stone's throw from the war-torn home they love. They sipped the elderflower cordial Merjema had brought, and I waited for them to get tired and tell me to stop. They didn't. I read into midnight. I read until the book was finished. When I closed it, Lejla held out her hand. She took a purple pen out of her satchel and drew a butterfly on the last page.

FRIDA RODRIGUEZ ... EN ROUTE

May 16, 1993
Paris, France

Fair Kate, who knew you could be such a bossy boots! But it worked. I wrote. So what do you think? Tell me the truth. Only if you like it. No! Tell me the truth no matter what. I know it needs context and explanations. Would anyone besides you want to read this? What's it even about? Food? Books? War? I tried to mention the library a few different ways. Did it work? I'm not sure about my voice. What about exclamation marks? They were a cardinal no-no in my journalism classes. Confession: They're my favorite punctuation mark! Hardly a secret, I know!!

I called it "The Ramona Club" because Merjema comes on Sundays now with Lejla. I make variations on the stew depending what's at the market and after we eat, I read to them. They're struggling with serious issues, but they still adore Beezus and Ramona. The other night we had a hilarious discussion about who we think we are. Lejla relates to wild child Ramona. No surprise there. Merjema is a responsible Beezus. I want to be a full-fledged Ramona but I have a feeling I'm a little of both. Which one are you?

You know how you said Bumpa will always be at Ye Olde

Curiosity Shop as long as the building exists? That got me thinking about other things that hold our memories — like books. Except books aren't anchored in one place like a building which means you can read a book that holds your memories anywhere. And food. If you can get your hands on the right ingredients, you can eat a dish that holds your memories anywhere too. If memories are inherent to our sense of identity, does that mean it's possible to reassemble parts of your identity no matter where you are in the world?

Ponderingly yours,

Frida

6/1/93

Dear Frida,

Wow! What a line: "No matter how bad food is, we taste it with generosity if it's made for us by a friend with a tender heart." And Branka's warm shiver laugh. And ending with the purple butterfly. Two thumbs up! Five stars! Ten! A lot of people would want to read this, but I know one person for sure: your mom.

Sometimes when you write to me, it's like our lives are in sync. Franny's up from Cali, and she came to the nursing home with Mom on Saturday. She's got lots of style and she's into the whole baby-doll dress look, so afterward we went shopping at The Bon. That led to a slumber party at my place. We were trying to decide what to have for dinner, and I swear I didn't prompt it, but we got into a conversation about food we remember and how it makes us think about certain people. It started with Aunt Wilma's chocolate chip cookies, and then Franny mentioned Aunt Norma's cinnamon rolls. The next thing we knew, it was like we were on an out-of-control episode of <u>Beat the Clock</u>, shouting things out. Aunt Judy's penuche! Aunt Janice's banana cream pie! Dad got his own whole bonus round. Monte Cristo sandwiches on Sundays! Chocolate malts at the Seahawks games!

I decided to tell them what you've been writing, about food memories and a sense of identity, and Mom told us that one of her first memories was sitting at the counter in the basement of Food Giant. Bumpa would buy a rib steak dinner for $1.49. Mom ate until she was full, and then he ate the rest. It was all he could afford, but she was little so she didn't realize it then. Whenever she sees rib steak on a menu, she says it reminds her how much she was loved. How bittersweet is that? Franny said peanut butter cookies make her think about how Mom sat with us in the kitchen after school and asked about our day, and I told them how Chef Boyardee pizzas in a box remind me of game nights and how we had fun together no matter where we lived.

That got us craving peanut butter cookies and one of those pizzas, so we made a run to Ballard Market. Don't laugh, but we make our cookies with a Betty Crocker cake mix. They really are the best. I wish I could say the same about the pizza. We even doctored it up with canned olives and mushrooms like Dad used to. Mom took the first bite. She started laughing and said, "You poor kids." Franny and I took bites, and it was <u>not</u> good. So how come that sour-tangy sauce made me feel so loved like Mom with the rib steak? We decided to call Dad and ask him what he remembered about the pizza, but when he picked up the phone, Mom giggled and said in a deep voice, "Hello, sir, is your refrigerator running?" and hung up on him. She crank called Dad! We laughed so hard I thought I was going to wet my pants. Then we ate that disgusting pizza and danced to "Sweet Caroline." I didn't think about Coleslaw Meatloaf or unexamined lives once all night.

Maybe it's a problem that I didn't mention any of this to Sven, but I don't feel like analyzing crank calls and Neil Diamond in the Big Scheme of Life. Just thinking about it fills my veins with molasses. So guess what? I won't think about it. I'm going to make a cup of chamomile tea and read Madeleine L'Engle. I'm starting the third book in her Crosswicks trilogy.

Your essay is amazing! You're amazing! Keep writing!

Lots of love,

Kate

P.S. I wish I was a Ramona. I'm definitely a Beezus.

P.P.S. I'm not sure what the Ramona Club will want to read next so I'm sending <u>From the Mixed-Up Files of Mrs. Basil E. Frank-weiler</u>, <u>The Phantom Tollbooth</u>, and <u>Charlotte's Web</u>.

FRIDA RODRIGUEZ ... EN ROUTE

June 14, 1993
Paris, France

Fair Kate,

Whew! RELIEF! You don't think my essay reeks. I'm not sure what it's going to be yet, but now that I've started I can't stop. I've written seventy-eight pages so far. Confession: I've been sneaking around behind your back. After all the grief I gave you about MFK there was no way I was going to ask you for more of her books so I slunk over to Shakespeare and Company and found <u>The Gastronomical Me</u> and <u>Two Towns in Provence</u>. Do Not Gloat! I get what you were telling me now about how whatever she writes feels like a natural part of who she is. That's how I want my writing to be. Not imitating hers but natural to me – minus the pinball punctuation. How come you didn't tell me MFK died last summer? You lost her <u>and</u> Laurie in a single year. You probably didn't tell me because I was such a jerk about her. I hope there's not an expiration date for apologies. Je suis désolée.

I'm not the crystals and woo-woo type but I do think we have some kind of cosmic connection and here's why. The other night the universe burst into our correspondence to make a point. Lejla showed up with flowered curtains from the flea market, and I told her how her gifts make my room feel like a sanctuary, but I feel guilty enjoying it when there are children in her country who can't even play outside without the risk of being shot.

Get this. She got mad at me. She says that kind of thinking is self-indulgent. We owe it to people who are suffering to savor everything good and beautiful we have in our lives. Not that we should deny bad things or turn our backs on them. But if suffering is contagious, then why isn't joy? Which virus do we want to spread? We don't help someone who's miserable by being miserable – we only add to the world's misery. Lejla knows her best friend's life is in genuine danger every single second, and she does one beautiful thing for someone every day to show the bad guys they're not winning. She lets herself feel joy so she can share joy. After all, you can't share something you don't have! I told her about you and she said don't waste time worrying about why you're dancing. Just keep dancing! Then I taught her how to make a crank call, but it turns out they don't really translate in French.

Cultivate beauty and joy, Fair Kate!

Frida

7/6/93

Dear Frida,

I want to spread joy, I do, but just when things are feeling steady, life pokes the beehive. Sven's parents didn't have time to celebrate his birthday this year, so I got some decorations at Pay 'n Save and made tomato pie and a well-intentioned but truly disgusting sugar-free cake. I used tinsel to turn my desk chair into a throne and presented his gift like the prince with Cinderella, but instead of the glass slipper, it was a pair of brown leather loafers he admired a few months ago at Kinney Shoes up at Northgate Mall. He stared at them for the longest time. Then he sobbed like there was no tomorrow. When I finally calmed him down, he told me how he came home from college one Christmas, and when the cab pulled up, his dad was standing in the living room window with his wrists slashed.

I froze. What do you say when someone tells you something like that? Sven called an ambulance, and they took his dad to Harborview. That's not even the worst part. His parents blamed him for his dad being committed to the psychiatric ward. They said he never should have called 911. He should have found another way to deal with it. Frida, his dad knew exactly what time he was getting in from the airport. The whole time Sven told me this, he kept thanking me for remembering how much he liked those shoes.

Did I tell you about last Valentine's Day? He gave me <u>The Oxford Companion to English Literature</u> because Margaret Drabble edited it, and he knows how much I love her. He gives the most thoughtful gifts, but somehow he can't begin to imagine anyone wanting to do anything thoughtful for him. It was just a pair of shoes, but he couldn't stop crying. I held him until he finally wore himself out. His whole body went limp. He whispered, "I expected them to behave like parents. Don't you see?" I asked him what he meant, and he said "disappointment" in the most forlorn voice I've ever heard.

When I woke up later, I looked down from the loft. He was sitting in the birthday throne reading Flaubert with a haze of lamplight around his golden curls. I used to spy on him reading like this and think he looked so peaceful, savoring a book in the quiet middle of the night. Now I know he's trying to read everything he can before he goes blind. He's trying to read his way out of his own reality.

This got me thinking. When I started reading authors I'd never heard of, I was sort of doing the same thing. I was trying to escape from myself and figure out how to be the next Anita Brookner or Penelope Lively or Muriel Spark because it's not like I have brainiac ideas or a screwy childhood to milk for inspiration. I didn't (still don't) fit in with the literary darlings like Mona Simpson and Donna Tartt, and I'll probably never have the faintest idea how to write something important like <u>A Lesson Before Dying</u> or <u>The Shipping News</u>. But I feel like something's changed lately.

Now with every book I read, I can feel myself figuring out how I can write in the way you describe. A way that's natural to me. I didn't tell you MFK died because there was so much else going on, but it makes sense you brought her up now. The store has a quarterly newsletter called "Book Bites," and for the anniversary of her death, I wrote an article about her legacy and how she captures the essence of human emotions through her reverence for daily pleasures (especially food) that most people take for granted. I know it's not fiction, but Emmett Watson praised my "splendid insight" in <u>The Seattle Times</u>. How <u>totally awesome</u> is that. He's one of the leading newspaper columnists in Seattle. A few people saw his mention and came into the store to talk to me like I'm an MFK expert or something. One of the times I was at the front counter with Kids Books Josephine and Caftan Dawn. Josephine said, "You captured old Mary Frances's spirit. Cheers to you, Perky." Now Dawn's not talking to her. Confession: Mr. Watson complimented <u>me</u> for <u>my</u> ideas about MFK, and I know it's not nice, especially after what I just told you about Sven's dad. I'm not taking that lightly, Frida, I'm really not, but part of me is selfishly pleased Sven had nothing to do with my article.

Love,

Kate

July 28, 1993
Paris, France

Fair Kate,

Poor Sven. And his poor dad. A person's despair has to run deep to do something harrowing like that. I get why Sven's on guard – that's not your average disappointment – can you imagine what it must feel like to spend your whole life waiting for the people you love to disappoint you like that? That's as depressing as spending your whole life trying not to disappoint the people you love. I should know! I la-di-da'd into a war for my sisters. A WAR! Not that I'm sorry I did. I know it's not as important as writing cover articles for <u>Current</u>, but I found a research fellow in Houston of all places who has microfiche of a collection of Turkish poems from the 1800s that was lost in the fire. He sent me a Xerox for one of Lejla and Irena's students.

You have no idea how glad I am to hear that you don't want to be any other writer except the One and Only Kate Fair. And of course Emmett Watson mentioned your article about MFK. You should be pleased you did it on your own, and that's NOT selfish!

Stupidity Confession: This one's about how we can royally disappoint ourselves. Guess who came back to town? Total Heathcliff relapse. Niko said he owed me an apology and took me out for a decadent meal at Port Alma. Sea bass in a salt crust with a creamy fennel gratin, a warm salad of langoustines, and a crisp bottle of Pouilly-Fumé. All of it overlooking the Eiffel Tower! I was fresh off my conversation with Lejla, so of course I savored happiness and beauty like it was my sworn duty.

Niko told me that having such successful parents makes him driven to live up to them. Isn't it scary how much of who you are depends on who randomly conceives you? Even now in his thirties he says it makes him selfish but he doesn't want to be like that – especially with someone like me. I bought it hook, line, and sinker. One thing led to another. Dot dot dot. We didn't leave each other's sides for three whole days! He promised to connect me with his editor at <u>Current</u>. All of a sudden I was going to be a War Journo Dame again. All of a sudden I forgot the reasons I'm not made to be a WJD. Stupid Frida because worst of all I completely forgot about the Ramona Club.

When I got back to the hotel on Sunday night my door was open. I heard voices and that's when I realized I ditched them for a hot guy like some desperate John Hughes character. I was too embarrassed to go in and tell them where I'd been, so I sat on the floor out in the hall. I could hear Merjema telling Kirby how she didn't want to leave Bosnia but her mother said, "You are the last hope for our family." Now she's here, but she can't get into a

French university because her transcripts are in Sarajevo, and the only way for her to get a work permit is to apply for political asylum. Kirby asked her how long that takes, and she told him it could be months so for now she cleans houses to survive.

Guys can be so different. Kirby listens and asks questions and listens some more, but Niko talked about himself for three days straight. When I told him about the Ramona Club, the only question he had was, "Why would you read kids' books?" Kirby read <u>Ramona the Pest</u> so he could talk to the Ramonas about it – that's what I've started calling Lejla and Merjema. How sweet is that? And he flipped out when you sent <u>The Phantom Tollbooth</u>. It was his favorite book when he was growing up. I almost forgot – can you send a copy of <u>Are You There God?</u> He wants to know what the fuss was about when girls were reading it back in junior high.

Sven doesn't know me, but would you give him a hug from me. I have a feeling he didn't get his fair share when he was growing up.

Stupidly yours,

Frida

P.S. I didn't tell Kirby about Niko. I don't think I should. What do you think?

From the smelly community room
at the Whispering Pines Nursing Home
for the last time

8/17/93

Dear Frida,

Don't beat yourself up about Niko. And definitely don't tell Kirby! Sweep that hunky mistake under the rug and move on. As for a copy of a lost poetry collection being less important than making the cover of <u>Current</u>, I bet that student you're helping disagrees.

Life is a giant seesaw. I can hardly believe how much it changes from one letter to the next. Bumpa is asleep for the night, and I suppose I should go home and write to you there. But I feel like staying a little longer to commemorate the Very Last Letter I ever write from this place. Farewell! Sayonara! Adios!

Mom and I got to talking on her last visit about how she hates leaving because she knows she won't be back for a week. It was like a lightbulb flashed on. Why in the heck is he in a nursing home up here? It's where he was taken after the hospital when we hoped he'd eventually go back to his trailer. But he's never going back to his trailer. We have to accept that. So why isn't he down in Olympia where she can visit him every day on her lunch break and weekends? Guess what? Bing-bang-boom! She found a new place. He's moving next week! You should have seen the grin on his face when she told him. He had his teeth in, and he looked like his old self.

Basking in joy,

Kate

P.S. You bet I'll send a copy of <u>Are You There God?</u> for Kirby. And it's totally (not crossed out) sweet that he read <u>Ramona the Pest</u> for the Ramonas.

Frida Rodriguez ... En Route

September 10, 1993
Paris, France

Fair Kate,

Such great news about Bumpa! I want to hear all about the new nursing home. Give me one of your signature Fair Kate descriptions.

So get this. When Lejla found out Kirby was reading Judy Blume, she invited him to join the Ramona Club. He asked if I was okay with it, and I told him if he doesn't mind the odd conversation about dealing with cramps in different cultures, it's a free world – sort of – join the party. But seriously, I'm glad she asked him, and not just because I like having him around. You should have seen him the first time he came. He showed up with a big straw tote like gnarled old Frenchwomen carry around the markets. He didn't say a word, just walked up to my hot plate, took a deep copper pot with a long handle out of the bag, and brought a little water to boil. He lowered the temp and poured in some coffee grounds. Then he added more water, showed Branka how to stir it quickly, and raised the heat until foam rose. It was like watching a mad scientist in his lab as he turned the heat down and up, letting the foam settle and rise again and then again.

I was so focused on what he was doing it took me a minute to notice his hands were trembling. Then I looked at his face. He was biting his lip he was concentrating so hard. He was nervous, Fair Kate. Kirby who always seems so at ease in the world! The spoon clattered against the demitasse cups when he scooped foam into them. I could tell by the way he was watching the Ramonas, he wanted everything to be perfect. Not to impress them or anything like that, but to make them happy. I started to get nervous for him like I did when Merjema was trying the bosanski lonac I made. Why were they so quiet? He set out a dish of sugar cubes and a plate of sweets. It was a Bosnian treat called rahat lokum. When Branka saw it, she squealed and shoved a piece in her mouth, and Lejla looked at him and said, "I think you are like Frida. You like to see me cry over food. Thank you, Kirby. You are a good man."

He turned ten shades of red and mumbled something about how Apple Cheeks at the Yugoslavian embassy made the rahat lokum in trade for borrowing his car so she could take a day trip to the Loire Valley. Then he got busy serving that brain-jangling coffee. It was magical the way the coffee coaxed memories into the room. Merjema told us how her grandma would open her kitchen window so the smell of freshly brewed coffee wafted outside and the neighbors knew it was time to come over and gossip. And when Lejla was little her dad dunked sugar cubes in his coffee and snuck them to her when her mom wasn't looking.

Kirby finally relaxed and described how on Lunar New Year his mom makes coffee the traditional Vietnamese way in little individual drip pots with sweet condensed milk.

I couldn't stop thinking about the effort he went to for the Ramonas – a few days later I took him to Le Mouffetard to thank him. The owners make their own brioches, and Kirby loves their hot apple tart with a café crème. To! Die! For! We talked more about Lunar New Year and the snacks his mom makes, like bánh chưng and pickled spring onions, and I realized for all the hours we've spent eating and gabbing, we've never talked about why his mom moved to America. Apparently we needed wine for that story, so we hopped over to Lisette's place.

I don't know much about Vietnamese history other than what I read in Martha's book. Kirby told me the country split in two in the 1950s. His mom's family lived in a village outside Hanoi, and the Communists burned down their house because they were Catholic landowners. They fled to the south. That's where she met his dad who was doing anthropology work for the University of Washington. Kirby said learning about what happened to his mom's house is what first got him interested in architecture and how physical spaces shape and hold our identities. He figured it could be a way to understand her better. When he told me that I thought – Lejla is right. He is a good man. I'm really lucky to have him in my life, Fair Kate.

By now we were starting in on our second carafe. All of a sudden I wanted to tell him about my writing. Of course he knows I write, but I don't really talk to him about it. Not the way we talk about everything else. I'm not sure why. But now I wanted to, so I explained some of my essays and how I've been thinking about food and books the way he thinks about architecture. He asked if he could read something, and I was tipsy enough to give him the photocopies I made for safekeeping. It seemed like a good idea at the time, but when I woke up – why do I care so much about what he's going to think?

Insecurely yours,

Frida

P.S. I forgot to tell you that after my last fiasco with Niko I decided to cut all ties, but piano-playing Bobbie has turned out to be a godsend. She actually got the letter I sent and called me when she came to Paris. Not only did she take three books back for us, she's going to try and get Merjema's university transcripts. She also said she'd check in on Irena. Irena gets messages to Lejla when she can but it's not enough. It's like their friendship is a nutrient – water or sun – and without it I can see Lejla physically wilting even though she tries so hard to stay positive. Bobbie said she'd do her best to get an update out to us once a week.

9/25/93

Dear Frida,

Of course you care what Kirby will think. He's one of your best friends. And he didn't go to all that thoughtful effort with the coffee just to please the Ramonas. Don't worry! He's going to love your writing. Especially the food stuff since you're both such fanatics.

I'm not really in the mood for describing, but here you go. Bumpa's new nursing home has nice personal touches like homemade quilts and a golden retriever named Abigail. And the gardens are going to radiate color when the rhodies and azaleas bloom in the spring. Not as bad as the last place, but it still smells like a nursing home, that icky combination of high school cafeteria gravy and all the Ensure they feed the patients. But it doesn't get me down because Mom visits Bumpa every day now, and that makes both of them so happy. Dad even picks him up on weekends sometimes and brings him out to the lake for a few hours.

It's strange not seeing Bumpa so much. I didn't realize how much time I spent thinking about visiting him and feeling guilty about not visiting him more. Knowing he's with Mom all the time opened up a lot of extra room in my mind, and I'm not sure it's a good thing. Like when I was rereading <u>Little Women</u> last weekend. It was one of my favorite books growing up, and when I got to the part where Jo goes to the newspaper office, it was like a time machine whooshed me back to my high school bedroom. Hippie fabrics all over everything, and I bought this steamer trunk at Kmart and pretended it was a coffee table to make my room look like an apartment. I even stuck candles in Chianti bottles. But the thing is I didn't just travel back to the physical space. My brain was fifteen again. I was writing a romance novel called <u>Seattle Blue</u>, and I felt exactly what it was like to be me then. Absolutely certain about who I was and what I wanted to write.

It got me remembering that Virginia Woolf assignment in college again, and Caftan Dawn telling Sven I won't have anything important to say until I'm forty, and now I'm obsessing about how I went from total self-confidence to feeling totally lost. I've started half a dozen short stories, and I'm spinning in circles. Frida, what if I don't find my way? Not even when I'm forty. Lately, it's like the bees are trapped under my skin buzzing around trying to escape. Sven's been asking me why I'm so grouchy lately, but I don't have the energy to get into it.

Love,

Kate

Frida Rodriguez ... En Route

October 7, 1993
Paris, France

Fair Kate,

The time has come for some Sally Jessy Raphael frank talk. Do you pay attention to what you write to me? Most of your letters lately have been about figuring things out. You've realized you don't want to be any other writer than you! You wrote a brilliant MFK article hailed by the esteemed Emmett Watson! You are NOT lost. You are on YOUR path. Your problem is that you still think of yourself as insecure. Stop it! Maybe you were when you first wrote to me, but now it's a Bad Habit. That's not who you are. At least it's not the Fair Kate I know.

I think one of the big reasons you're grouchy is because it's too much work holding Sven at arm's length. I know I'm hardly one to talk – Leap Before You Look Frida – but think about how it must make him feel. His parents don't know how to be parents. His novel is dying. He's afraid of going blind. Here you are getting your life sorted out, and you won't even tell him about dancing to Neil Diamond. Seriously, Kate, if you let him all the way in he'll get to see not everyone's going to let him down and maybe he'll stop harping about disappointment and he might even cut back on his exhausting arguments about the meaning of everything. Isn't it worth a shot? Nine out of ten kitchen table therapists approved this message.

Your Sage Parisian Amiga,

Frida

10/24/93

Dear Sally Jessy,

That was an impressive reprimand. I appreciate the frank talk even though the fog is thicker than ever. Before I could even think about taking Sven down to see Bumpa, everything took a hard right turn. He's up for a job with a literary foundation in New York. If he gets it he'll host their reading series like he does here, but more than that because basically he'll run their whole author program. It's perfect for him. He keeps in touch with so many writers who read at the store. Last week he got letters from Mary Morris (she asked how <u>my</u> writing is going!) and Melanie Rae Thon (she's struggling to figure out whether a story she's working on should start at the beginning or the end, and she asked for his advice).

The night before he flew out for his interview, we splurged on two big crabs from Pike Place and managed not to ruin them. We nearly made ourselves sick with all the melted butter, not to mention a whole bottle of Gato Negro. If he gets the job, he says I won't have to work. I can just write my stories. I'd love to live in New York, but Confession: I want to live in <u>Barefoot in the Park</u>

not <u>Bright Lights, Big City</u>. Sometimes I feel like I'm not in the groove of my own times.

When I told Sven New York intimidates me, he said, "But someone must take Laurie Colwin's place." I didn't ruin the moment by telling him I don't want to take anyone's place, not even my beloved Laurie's. The night was blissfully domestic. I showed him how to roll his shirts in his suitcase so they won't wrinkle. We talked about what it would be like to raise children in a place like New York with all the museums and culture. We fell asleep tangled up on the love seat reading. Him: Andre Dubus. Me: Ann Hood.

He called last night to tell me about having dinner with a guy named Chip who's the managing editor at <u>The New Yorker</u>. Chip was a student in one of John L'Heureux's writing classes. John adores Sven and made the introduction. They talked about some of Sven's stories, and Chip said he'd consider them. I'm thrilled for him, Frida. This is his unsung song. It's the life he's meant to live ~~if he doesn't~~.

He's staying with a friend from college for two weeks so he can make publishing connections, and ~~since he's been gone I've felt less~~ I've been keeping busy. Kids Books Josephine is hell-bent on expanding my palate and introduced me to tom kha gai and spanakopita. And I went to Il Bistro in Pike Place with some other booksellers. We drank too much rioja and played truth or dare but really it was just truth. Travel Section Jane told us how she gets stomach cramps when she's anxious, and the first thing Fiction Section Polly does on vacation is buy a trashy romance from the Loveswept series. Jane seems like the last person in the world to have anxiety, and I never dreamed Polly would be into bodice rippers, so I fessed up to my buzzing bees and love affair with Danielle Steel. It was surprising to find out how much we have in common.

Another night Stella and I spent an hour at Blockbuster trying to decide what movie to rent. She wanted <u>Wild at Heart</u>. I wanted <u>The Fabulous Baker Boys</u> since Sven isn't into movies like that. We ended up playing pool instead. There's this pool hall called the 211 Club in Belltown. It's all serious old men like <u>The Color of Money</u>. There's a sign on the wall that says, "No Music, No Whistling, No Bulls***, Just Pool." (They spell out the word.) We're not great players, but we're not bad, either. It was fun to shoot a few rounds and sit at the bar. We were the only girls there, and no one bugged us except once the bartender shushed us because we laughed too loud.

Afterward we walked over to Septieme for tea. I'm careful not to talk about Sven with anyone at the store. It's Gossip Central there. But Stella and I have been getting closer, and I told her a little bit which ended up leading to a lot. She said maybe he's the way he is not because his life has been full of more horrible incidents. Maybe it's the emphasis he places on those incidents. I told her it's hard for me to judge because look at the life I've been given compared to his. I don't have his parents. I don't have diabetes. But Stella said that's not an excuse and opened up to me about her childhood. Frida, it was heart-wrenching. But you can tell she doesn't sit around waiting for people to disappoint her even more.

I asked her what she thinks about Lejla's idea that it's our duty to feel joy. She didn't hesitate. She said, "Of course! Like the world needs any more agony." The next night Roy and I had drinks at Larry's Greenfront, and we started talking about it, too. I wondered if it's truly possible to spread joy or if we just tell ourselves we can so we don't feel guilty for having a good time when a Black Hawk crashes in Mogadishu and U.S. soldiers are dragged through the streets. Roy asked if I've heard of the Butterfly Effect. There's actually a line about it in The Phantom Tollbooth. The Princess of Pure Reason tells Milo, "Whatever we do affects everything and everyone else, if even in the tiniest way. Why, when a housefly flaps his wings, a breeze goes round the world." Roy says life is hard enough without making it harder on purpose. If we're going to flap our wings and send breezes, they should at least be refreshing ones. Of course I thought about Lejla's purple butterflies.

It was interesting to talk to Stella and Roy about this, but it made me realize I've never brought it up with Sven because he'd disagree and hound me to admit he's right, and I'd eventually agree because he's better at words than me. There's this part in A Circle of Quiet where Madeleine writes about how the more limited our language is, the more it restricts our power to think. My language still feels so limited when I try to express what I'm thinking. Maybe that's the real reason I haven't let Sven all the way in and why I don't tell my parents how lost I can feel off the boat. Because I'm still figuring out how to explain it to myself.

Talking to Stella and Roy also made me realize how much I

wish I was in Paris. I LOVE our letters, but there's something different about everyday friends you spend time with. If I was in Paris we could go to the flea market and cram things into Kirby's mini car. Or take Branka to the Rodin garden and look at snails with brown stripes on their shells. Or sit in Chez Lisette overlooking the Seine and drink wine and spill joy all over the place. Wishfully yours,

Kate

P.S. We just found out that Forth & Regal plans to put a superstore in the Lamonts building in U Village. Kay's Bookmark is in that mall. How predatory is that!

FRIDA RODRIGUEZ ... EN ROUTE

November 14, 1993
Paris, France

Dear Kate,

I can't believe you mentioned <u>The New Yorker</u>. Can you say coincidence? But first – more frank talk. I thought the issue with Sven was only with your family, but it's your whole life isn't it? I'm expanding on what I wrote in my last letter. Take Serious Sven to play pool with Stella. Talk to him about romance novels with Fiction Section Polly. And get him down to the nursing home so you can show him how doing macrame is REAL happiness. If you can't share your whole life with him, you're going to be fragmented forever and that's going to make you miserable and who wants to be miserable so you might as well break up with him. Not that I'm saying break up with him. What I'm saying is break up with your Bad Habit! Ha – sometimes I exhaust myself with my cleverness.

But what's all this about <u>The New Yorker</u>, Frida? Patience, Fair Kate. Follow the bouncing ball. I came back to my room a few days ago and found a note slipped under my door. It said, "I read your pages. Meet me at Lisette's at eight." A bass drum thudded in my stupid tender heart. First of all, Kirby had had the pages for weeks and nary a word. I felt like there was an elephant in the room every time we hung out together. Second of all, the only reason he would want to talk in public is so I wouldn't cry when he told me how awful my writing is. I arrived to find him at our favorite table with a carafe of Chablis at the ready and moules marinières on the way. If that doesn't scream last meal, what does? But when Kirby set my pages on the table between us, he raised his glass of wine and said, "It's honest. It's humanizing. It's strong and vulnerable all at the same time. Like you, Frida."

I felt like I'd been holding my breath ever since I gave him those essays. I opened my mouth to say thank you, and I couldn't believe it. I burst into tears. He just put his hand over mine and let me cry. Am I an idiot, Kate? How have I been so blind? He's smart. He's attractive. He's a really, really good man. He was looking at me, and I couldn't tell how he felt. Am I just a friend? Did I ruin any chance of something more back when we had our big fight? I was sure he could hear my heart pounding, but before I could say something irreparably awkward and stupid, he handed me an envelope and said, "I'm not done."

I opened it to find a letter to him from someone named Lauren. Let me paraphrase. Dear Kirby – salutations, niceties, etc. – sorry it took me so long – busy this, busy that – your friend Frida sounds like she has a valuable story to tell – the Ramona Club – intrigued – please put us in touch. Paul sends his love.

So who is this Lauren Dunne you ask. Kirby's college roommate's wife who is on the editorial staff at – finally – <u>The New Yorker</u>! My heart pounded for all sorts of new reasons now. Kirby thought my writing was good enough to tell Lauren about. Lauren thought it sounded good enough to follow up. I felt dizzy. Kirby said he had some thoughts and asked me if I'd like to hear them. Of course! He had interesting suggestions for making The Ramona Club essay stand on its own without clogging it with too much exposition. We talked about it for so long Lisette finally gave us a key to lock up and went home.

And because I know it's on your mind – no, we didn't kiss. You can bet I thought about it, but what if his head wasn't in the same space as mine? I can't ruin our friendship. I just can't.

The next morning I sent a letter to Lauren Dunne. I have a good feeling about this. Did I just jinx myself? I hope not. Anticipatingly yours!
Frida

P.S. I'm jealous of your everyday friends! I wish you were in Paris too. Come visit me!

P.S. Deux. Los Angeles is lucky. Dutton's, Pickwick's, Small World, Book Soup, Vroman's, Chevalier's, Dawson's, Hollywood Book City – we have too many great local bookstores for a greedy superstore to do any harm.

P.S. Trois. I think you could really thrive in New York, and don't worry – if you end up going, I know you'll find a version of the city that's just right for you.

11/28/93

Dear Frida,

I have to admit I've been wondering when you'd finally catch on to how perfect Kirby is for you. He really is, Frida. And I bet you anything he feels what you're feeling, too. But I get why you're cautious. I think that's smart as long as you're not too cautious, okay? And in the meantime: <u>The New Yorker</u>! Obviously I was excited for Sven, but this is a whole other level. Talk about the year of woman power. Toni Morrison wins the Nobel, Ruth Bader Ginsburg becomes a Supreme Court justice, and FRIDA RODRIGUEZ IS HEADED FOR <u>THE NEW YORKER</u>. Finally, the world is getting something right!! Let me know ASAP when they accept you because obviously they will.

I'm down at Mom and Dad's house in Olympia, and you'll be thrilled to know that I ditched my caution, and Sven spent Thanksgiving with us before he hopped on the plane and made his Big Move to the Big Apple. I did it, Frida. I brought my worlds together, and nothing collapsed. I'm moving to New York once Sven gets settled. But first, let me set the stage for Thanksgiving on Summit Lake.

Envision a polished powder-blue sky. Alder and birch leaves

shine like caramelized honey amidst the cool evergreen trees. It's a perfect autumn day. Franny is up from Cali again. Bumpa's sister and brother-in-law (my Great-Aunt Irene and Great-Uncle Paul) are down from Snohomish. The nursing home made it possible for Bumpa to spend the entire day with us, and Dad and Sven carried his wheelchair onto the deck. Bumpa lived so much of his life on the water. It's his Happy Place, and there he was on the lake in one of his old windbreakers and fishing hats!

Franny was in the kitchen with Mom and Great-Aunt Irene doing whatever it is people do to a turkey. Dad, Sven, and I were on lawn chairs with Bumpa chatting and reading. Sven had John Casey's <u>Spartina</u>. How appropriate is that? I was feeling a little anxious, but then I heard the sliding glass door open behind us and the deep vibrating hum of the organ. Great-Uncle Paul started playing "I Left My Heart in San Francisco," and Bumpa's head tilted toward the music. He loves listening to Great-Uncle Paul play, and the most serene look came over his face. It felt like our old Thanksgivings at their house when Bumpa and Great-Aunt Irene's brothers were alive. And Sven was there to be a part of it! My heart was a big goopy joyous Laurie Colwin–esque mess.

For dinner we had a très elegant dish that I'm positive never graced the Rodriguez holiday table: Fair Family Orange Jell-O Salad with Pineapple and Shredded Carrots. To heck with <u>Gourmet</u>'s cornmeal stuffing with pancetta, walnuts, and dried cherries. Dad sauteed canned mushrooms for his bread stuffing. Of course anxiety tried to make a Grand Entrance when we sat down to eat. What if everyone started telling family stories, and Sven felt left out or thought we were trivial? What if he started a conversation about one of his Big Ideas (unexamined lives or quiet desperation), and everyone looked at him like he just landed from Pluto? I feel like an idiot, Frida. He was so charming, especially to Great-Aunt Irene, and he loved all the stories. Even the one about the time she and Bumpa were riding a horse into their barn. She was in front and saw the beam up ahead and ducked, but she forgot to warn Bumpa. He hit that beam straight on. It knocked him out cold. Is it weird that we never get tired of a story like that? It's not even very interesting, but we crack ourselves up, and I don't know if I've ever seen Sven laugh so hard.

Later when we were bundled up on the dock looking at the stars, he thanked me for sharing my family with him. He said he can't wait to make our own memories and drive our kids crazy repeating them over and over someday. It felt like the right time to tell him Lejla's theory about our duty to savor everything beautiful in our lives, not to protect ourselves but because it can make a difference. You won't believe his response. He said, "I'm beginning to understand." I almost fell off the dock. ~~All my stupid fears~~ Thank you for pushing me.

Love,

Kate

Frida Rodriguez ... En Route

December 22, 1993
Paris, France

Dear Kate,

Congratulations! You did it! You let Serious Old Sven in! I don't want to say I told you so, but the Fairest of Kates in All the Land – boy oh boy did I tell you so! I'm over the moon for me. Ha! New York is SO much closer to Paris than Seattle.

Now about this Kirby situation. Even if I decided to throw caution to the wind, it's not like I can make any smooth moves right now anyway because he went to Vietnam for Christmas. And before he left it was business as usual except for the $100 bottle of Champagne he bought – yes you read that right! – when glamorous Lauren Dunne got back to me. She thinks I have the potential for an article about how war displaces a sense of identity, but I need to decide on my anchoring incident. The night the library burned? That first night of the Ramona Club? My goal is to get as close as I can and then Lauren will help me. Isn't that what editors are for?

Speaking of the Ramona Club. We're growing. Lejla brought two more refugee students, and I felt bad because I kept borrowing a hot plate from my neighbor Faith, so I invited her to join us.

Her parents fled the Nigerian-Biafran war in the late 1960s, and she grew up in Montreal. She's apprenticing with a sculptor named Niki de Saint Phalle who makes art to raise awareness about AIDS. Is there anyone in Paris who isn't très intéressant? Apple Cheeks from the Yugoslavian embassy is part of our group now, too. Faith is a proud Beezus. Apple Cheeks is a closet Ramona.

A week or so ago everyone asked me to make a Mexican dish. My first thought was – obviously – chiles rellenos. It was an ordeal in and of itself to get the ingredients. Kirby had to track down an agriculturalist out by Versailles who has been experimenting with peppers in greenhouses, and even then I had to substitute. I got the idea that rather than prepare it by myself, we'd all make it together. Two hot plates weren't going to cut it, so I asked Lisette if we could use the bistro kitchen when she's closed. There were ten of us. It was like that old <u>Life</u> magazine photo of people crammed into a VW Bug. I usually hate people in my way when I'm cooking but this was a blast. We had a contest to see who could separate eggs without leaving the slightest drop of yolk. Merjema won. Her aunt has a bakery and sometimes Merjema helped her make orašnice, which is a kind of cookie made with egg whites, walnuts, and sugar. She told us when she was six, she lost a tooth in the orašnice batter. She was too scared to tell her aunt, and the next day a woman came in and plunked the tooth on the counter. From then on customers would say, "I'll take an order of orašnice please, hold the tooth."

How do you like my responsible use of commas above? I might be a <u>New Yorker</u> writer soon. I take that seriously!.

You know how judgy I was growing up because Mom wrote about food when she could have been writing about More Important Things. Cooking in Lisette's kitchen with the Ramonas – it struck me in a new way, what Mom does. Wipe that look of satisfaction off your face! How come I could never see how she uses food to tell people's stories – and by telling their stories explore their cultures – and by exploring their cultures explain their lives in a way everyone can understand because everyone eats. Everyone eats! I thought that's the reason it wasn't a Big Deal but Mom understands that's the reason it IS a Big Deal! No gloating, Fair Kate!

Did I ever tell you how she got on a freighter all by herself when she was our age and traveled to Asia to write about food – she still calls it the Orient, and I keep telling her she <u>can't</u> say that anymore. She's been to India six times and Thailand four for work. She's been to every state in Mexico – and written about all of them so people in L.A. can know about those places and even experience them because she includes recipes. If a flavor can take me home, why can't a flavor take me someplace I've never been? Why can't it take me inside someone's life where I can see how much we have in common – how we all just want to be nourished – even if it feels like we're polar opposites on the surface?

I wrote her a letter, Fair Kate. I told her I'm sorry for being so disrespectful about what she does. If you get to thank me for pushing you to let Sven in, I get to thank you for standing your ground with MFK so I could see Mom in a different light.

Flavorfully yours,

Frida

1/20/94

Dear Frida,

While I might enjoy gloating a teensy-tiny bit about Kirby (perchance absence will make the heart grow fonder), I'd never gloat about your mom. I'm proud of you for apologizing. And it ties in to an interesting conversation I had with Franny on the phone the other night. I was telling her how I worry I'll always be playing catch-up because I didn't think about life's Big Ideas when I was growing up. She said don't be silly. No one has Big Ideas when they're young. That's what our twenties are for. I bet a few of my fellow booksellers who read Thomas Hardy in their bassinets would disagree, but it made me wonder. Maybe our twenties are also for having Big Conversations with our parents that we couldn't have when we were kids, because when we were kids they were too busy raising us and we were too busy being raised to really understand them.

This is probably on my mind because Confession: I haven't told Mom and Dad I'm moving to New York. I can never seem to find the right time, and it's not like Sven and I have even decided on the exact date for me to join him. I don't know why but whenever I think about telling them, ~~it feels like~~ Once again, I'm at a loss for words. The store feels off-kilter with Sven gone, but I don't have much time to miss him when I'm working. I have another new role. Do you know what a book club is? It's when a group of people reads the same book every month and meets to talk about it. Our night manager K2 (that's her nickname) started a program where book clubs can come in and a bookseller helps them plan their reading list for the year. A few weeks ago, she chose me to be one of those booksellers. I don't know if I've mentioned her before, but she always knows how to pick the exact right book for a person, so it's a real honor.

We have a regular list of store recs like <u>The Joy Luck Club</u>, <u>Beloved</u>, and <u>Housekeeping</u>, and all the clubs have been reading <u>A Thousand Acres</u> ever since it came out in paperback. But I also get to suggest my own choices. I already got three clubs to add <u>Moon Tiger</u>. It's surreal, Frida. I stand in front of groups of well-read women, and they want to hear what I have to say. The other night I explained why <u>The All of It</u> is great for discussions (it centers on a moral dilemma, in case you're dying of curiosity). I didn't once feel like an imposter. Between book clubs and special orders, I've become an essential part of the store.

Sven stocked up on phone cards, and he calls at least every other day. He can't wait to take me to browse used books at the Strand, and he says our new Lombardi's is a place called Gene's in Greenwich Village where he finally found a nice apartment he can afford. (That's the main reason we hadn't set a date for my move.) We wanted a brownstone. I love that word. It sounds so New York. But Confession: Thinking about moving is making me feel sentimental about my little Ballard burrow.

It's so cozy here in the winter. On my days off I read (Anita and Penelope have new novels out) and cook (I'm working on this enchilada recipe from <u>Gourmet</u> that has spinach in it). Even though my windowsill garden is desolate this time of year, a while back I bought vases to force bulbs. I arranged them on a shelf in my closet (they need dark to get their start), and every morning I peek in and see the roots reaching a little deeper into the water. When I looked today, a few of the bright green stems are starting to dimple at their tips. I can't remember which ones are hyacinths and which ones are paper whites, and I haven't felt this kind of anticipation since the night before Christmas when I was a kid. I need to keep reminding myself that I can force bulbs in a New York closet, too.

Love,

Kate

P.S. Go to the American Express office on rue Scribe. I hope you like my surprise. I'll explain in my next letter.

FRIDA RODRIGUEZ ... EN ROUTE

February 13, 1994
Paris, France

Fair Kate,

I couldn't believe it when the guy at AmEx handed me the envelope. $600! How? Booksellers don't make that kind of dough. I put Lejla in charge of it and she put Faith in charge because she says Faith is impartial, plus she has one of those new digital notebooks with a program called Quicken for keeping track of money. Faith is working with the Ramonas to figure out priorities. A rent fund? Food? Cotton candy from the cart at the Eiffel Tower? That request is Branka's. They're so moved by your generosity – especially since it feels like the siege is never going to end.

What's the Clinton administration thinking? Operation Provide Santa? A lot of good fifty tons of air-dropped toys and kids' clothes will do when innocent people are STILL being shot in the streets! I don't get how people can care so much about Tonya Harding when the Serb forces bombed another market and killed sixty-eight people.

I'm struggling with my essay. I can't believe it's been more than a year since I was in Bosnia. I'm still wrapping my head around what happened when I was there. The Nazis burned twenty million books, but that wasn't all in one place. About two million books and special collections were destroyed in one single night in Sarajevo. I've tried writing from different angles, but I'm not capturing what it really felt like. I know I'm not going to be a WJD, but I picked up <u>The Face of War</u> again. It's different now that I've actually been in a war because I can understand that there was only so far Martha could take me into the experience. And she had to do it exactly right, guiding my imagination to the feelings that are impossible to put into words. That's the real skill, Kate. Leading the reader to their own empathy beyond yours so it has meaning for them and stays with them when they finish reading.

Fine – gloat about Kirby! You have every right to since I'm missing him like some kind of maniac. He decided to stay in Vietnam for the Lunar New Year, and I can't tell you how many times I've caught myself walking down the hall to his room to tell him something before I remember he's gone. Every time it happens, a wave of melodramatic emotions washes over me, like I'm one of those pining heroines in the romance novels you read in junior high. Enough said!

Congratulations on being an essential part of the bookstore. I'm not surprised. I told you from the start. You have more going for you than knowing how to wrap a gift.

I want to tell you that having the New York convo with your

parents will be no big deal, but I'm not in any shape to give family-related reassurances right now. Mom hasn't responded to my letter. Do you think she hates me?

Uneasily yours,

Frida

3/15/94

Dear Frida,

Greetings from a typical sopping Seattle spring day. When I left the apartment for work, I noticed tiny green leaves sprouting on the lilac bush across the street. I feel like I measure the rhythms of my life by that bush. Leaves, buds, blossoms, bare branches, and then it starts all over again. So much has happened since I watched the leaves sprout last year. I wonder where my life will be when the lilacs are in bloom this year?

Your mom doesn't hate you. Don't say that! You're my idol for being honest with her. I wish I was fearless like you. And wise. What you wrote about guiding people to their own empathy. That's exactly what you do with your writing because you're not afraid to wear your tender heart on your sleeve. People say that like it's a bad thing, but why? Look how you use it to help readers (me) understand (and feel) what other people are going through.

You're right about booksellers not making "that" kind of money. I was doing my weekly prowl in the basement at Bowie & Company, and I came across a book called <u>We Followed Our</u>

<u>Stars</u>. It's an autobiography of a woman named Ida Cook. She and her sister used their passion for opera as a cover to get Jewish people out of Germany at the start of WWII. It's appropriate that you mentioned romance novels, because she made the money to do it by writing those exact kinds of novels under the pen name Mary Burchell.

As you well know I was painfully embarrassed when I got out into the Real World and found out Everyone But Me grew up on <u>Middlemarch</u> while I was reading Harlequins. It turns out Ida aka Mary wrote one of those Harlequins. How do I know this? Because I kept it. <u>Under the Stars of Paris</u>. Why did I keep it? I have no idea. I headed straight to the library, and a marvelous librarian (aren't they all) helped me hunt through microfiche and reference books. We tumbled down the rabbit hole and discovered all these amazing things about Ida. She was honored as Righteous Among the Nations by the World Holocaust Remembrance Center in Israel, <u>and</u> she was president of the Romance Novelists' Association. She wrote in their newsletter how a bad romantic novel is embarrassing and indefensible, but so is a bad realistic novel, plus the bad realistic ones are usually pretentious, too. Then she added, "But a good romantic novel is a heartwarming thing which strikes a responsive chord in those who are happy and offers a certain lifting of the spirits to those who are not."

Her words keep circling in my brain. A certain lifting of the spirits. You do that, Frida. But what spirits do I lift? It breaks my heart, the thought of Merjema cleaning houses when she should be in school. It's not the Ramonas' fault they had to flee their country. And what am I doing other than feeling bad about it? I thought about Ida, unapologetically writing her romantic novels so she could make the world a better place, and I asked if we could hold a fundraiser at the store. We'd invite the book clubs we work with and donate 10% from their purchases to my new project: Book Clubs for Bosnia.

I was hoping we'd make at least $100, but after I gave a short speech about the Ramona Club, all the women donated an extra $5 or $10 when they bought their books. The people working downstairs in the café gave us everything out of their tip jar, and remember Caftan Dawn? She apologized for saying I wasn't good enough for Sven. She said she was going through a hard time with her husband and feeling bad about herself, and she took it out on me. Then she gave me $55. I felt awful for my mean thoughts about her. Everyone has a story. You never know what it is or why it makes them do the things they do. Misjudge not lest ye be misjudged!

Love,

Kate

Frida Rodriguez ... En Route

Fair Kate,

The Ramonas had a soaking wet weepathon when I told them about Book Clubs for Bosnia. And my own waterworks went into overdrive when I finally got Mom's letter. You're right. She doesn't hate me. She told me how much my apology meant to her. The sickening part was I could tell it surprised her. Not that I misjudged her but that I was sorry for misjudging her. That made me feel like the worst daughter in the world. Especially since she wrote how after she got her master's degree she wanted to write about social problems but the only jobs the newspapers would offer her were in the women's sections writing about hemlines and food. Women weren't given serious opportunities back then. But after a while she realized the day-to-day people she met were as important as Dulles and de Gaulle. Maybe even more important. She wrote, "There's more peace to be made over a curry buffet than at a treaty table." She discovered she could actually tell people's stories in a deeper way than if she was a regular reporter. A reporter gives ONLY facts, but through food she gets to write about curiosity, passion, hope, and every other human emotion you can think of. I never knew she was so proud of her job. Whose fault is that? Misjudge not indeed!

Speaking of. You're sorely misjudging yourself if you don't think you do anything to lift people's spirits. Let's start with Bumpa. Not every granddaughter would drive all over town buying macrame supplies. And what about how you work so hard to find just the perfect books for people. Not to mention my mixtape which I play whenever I get a case of the Gloomy Gerties.

I'm cutting this short because I have a computer class today. I'm learning a program called FileMaker Pro so I can make a database of all the universities I've contacted.

Nonjudgmentally yours,

Frida

The end of the world as I knew it

4/16/94

Dear Frida,

I wish I wrote to you two days ago like I'd planned to do before I got sucked into <u>The Girls of Slender Means</u>. That would have been a cheerful letter about your mom and how life has a nice way of falling into place. But Frida, it's not true. Muriel Spark was interrupted by a long call from Sven, and then it was time to make lunch for Stella. I thought I'd take a break from tomato pie and have some fun. I made the tater tot casserole that likes to make an appearance at family potlucks. Cream of mushroom soup and tons of gooey cheese. I thought Stella would get a kick out of that. I unfolded my little IKEA table, and a new batch of hyacinths are in bloom, so I put a purple one between our plates. I added a green salad with dried cranberries and a bottle of Gato Negro, and I could have been Laurie Colwin's protégé if I wasn't feeling so low.

I told Stella how Sven called because he was upset. His boss reprimanded him for overstepping bounds with some of the program's authors by asking them to read <u>Into the Liminal Gloaming</u> and recommend it to their agents. He even asked Norman Mailer. Then there are the stories he keeps writing for <u>The New</u>

<u>Yorker</u>. So far Chip hasn't wanted any of them. He calls them too lugubrious. But that's not the kick in the gut. Stella said, "What about the Thanksgiving story? That was a good one." I didn't know what she was talking about, and the second she realized this, I could tell something was wrong.

It makes me sick thinking about it. I just walked away and made myself a cup of chamomile tea, but it's not helping. Sven wrote a story about our Thanksgiving weekend, and he sent it to Stella even though they're barely friends and he knows she and I are good friends. She assumed I knew. She gave it to me at work yesterday. He made that day seem so ~~insignificant dingy~~ insignificant and dingy. My head is going to explode! I'd Xerox it for you but I was so furious I ran upstairs to our accounting office and shoved it in the shredder. It doesn't matter. I can still see the words. Sludge of Jell-O! Cramped idea of family! The groan of arthritic fingers on the organ's reluctant keys! How dare he!!! Those keys vibrated with joy when Great-Uncle Paul's nimble fingers played "Beautiful Dreamer." Sven was genuinely laughing WITH us when we told our family stories. I'm positive he was. ~~So why would he~~ Frida, you should have heard him on the phone trying to defend himself. He said he borrowed a few details to flesh out a modern-day allegory. Allegory about what?? You can guess where that question went. When he careened onto the quiet desperation highway, I slammed the phone down so hard I cracked the receiver.

~~I couldn't feel my~~ The next thing I knew I was ripping books off my shelves. My hands flew, building a nest in the middle of the floor. I curled up inside it and waited for the sobs to come, but the strangest thing happened. My ladies started rising up. Penelope, Anita, Iris, Margaret, Muriel, the Brontë sisters, Edith, MFK, Virginia, Louisa May, Madeleine, Laurie. They circled in closer and cradled me. I opened <u>An Accidental Man</u> and Iris said, "It is just that I am not in my right place in the universe. And if I married you, I would be increasingly not in my right place, and this would be true to eternity no matter how happy we were together." All those nights Sven and I read to each other. Those were truly happy times, Frida. But he wasn't my right place, was he?

Huddled inside my shelter of books, everything became clear. Sven wrote that story to prove his point. Being disappointed by the one you love is inevitable. Disappointing the one you love is inevitable. He sabotaged his own happiness to beat disappointment to the punch. Maybe not even consciously, but that might make it worse. He actually belittled Jell-O to make his life more meaningful. What kind of person has hostility toward Jell-O? He's so damn desperate for it to mean Something that he was here on this earth. God forbid playing the organ for your sick brother-in-law might be as significant as writing a Great American Novel That Articulates The Meaning Of Life! But what if it is, Frida? Those songs transported Bumpa out of his illness, like the food you make for the Ramonas transports them out of their sorrow.

I'm a zombie. I don't know what to do.

. . . And then I did it. I called Sven and told him I'm not going to New York. I deleted him from my speed-dial and erased every single one of his messages on my answering machine. There's so much more I want to write, but I'm too sad.

Love,

Kate

FRIDA RODRIGUEZ ... EN ROUTE

April 25, 1994
Paris, France

Oh Kate, I feel awful. I pushed you to let Sven in acting like I'm some wise old woman. I'm obnoxious. I shouldn't have given him so much benefit of the doubt. This is all my fault. Here's my dirty secret. I expect – in my heart of hearts – people to be honorable. Like you! Your kindness created a chain reaction. Lisette is now donating part of her profits every Saturday – her busiest day – to the Ramonas, and the Village Voice bookstore is hosting a fundraiser. People are going to take turns reading passages from MFK Fisher's last book.

Sometimes when I'm writing to you a thought pops into my head and it could only happen <u>because</u> I'm writing to you. Like right now I'm suddenly thinking about MFK and her first marriage to Al. He was brilliant like Sven. Tortured too. She had to be with him, but then she had to leave him to find herself. What if no matter how wrong they are for us, we need to love some people so we can grow – and then outgrow them like MFK outgrew Al? What if that's the whole reason they come into our lives? So we can grow with them and then beyond them. I know how much Sven was part of your dreams. Maybe he still is. Just not the way you thought he was going to be. Or maybe this is Guilty Frida's way of defending herself for shoving you into that train wreck.

Apologetically yours,

Frida

THE PUGET SOUND BOOK COMPANY

101 South Main Street   Seattle, WA 98104

5/5/94

Dear Frida,

Sven sends me at least a letter a day. In the last one he wrote, "I hate this part. I don't want to let you go." He did love me. I'm sure of it. As much as he was able to. And I truly believe he wants to be happy. I want him to be happy, but how can he be when he has such damaged ideas about what happiness is? That's what makes me even sadder. I told Stella what you said about outgrowing people, and she said when she broke up with her high school boyfriend, she had to do it in order to continue growing. We decided this is the most painful reason of all to end a relationship, because it doesn't mean you stopped loving someone. It means you're no longer being fed in a way that nourishes you, and if you don't leave, you'll slowly starve to death. In the beginning with Sven, every day was a feast, but by the end, I was so hungry all the time. I wonder when it was, the precise point when we crossed the borders from what we were going to become to what we couldn't become to what we didn't become.

None of this was your fault, Frida. That would mean it never should have happened, and I don't believe that.

Love,

Kate

P.S. Is Kirby back from Vietnam?

FRIDA RODRIGUEZ ... EN ROUTE

May 15, 1994
Paris, France

Fair Kate,

I guess the days of Saran Wrapping a guy's car after a breakup are long gone. You're being so mature. Think about it. If you and a guy like Sven broke up back when I first met you, you would have been positive it was because you were an idiot. Obviously, I'm not saying you were. I'm saying that's what you would have thought. Now you can see you broke up because you weren't the right people for each other. That's Oprah-worthy self-awareness.

I'm writing to you from a little café in Place Dauphine over-looking the soft pink blossoms of the chestnut trees. It's warm but not too warm, and I ordered a citron pressé. Is there any more refreshing drink in the world? Mais non! Can you believe it's my third spring in Paris? My first spring here without Kirby. That's why I'm not at Chez Lisette. Too many associations to distract me while I ponder the letter he just sent. He's staying in Vietnam. Clinton lifted the trade embargo, and Kirby wants to study how French colonial architecture affected the Vietnamese sense of cultural identity. He says he has to act fast before the American investment tsunami crashes into the country to take advantage of cheap Communist labor. I love the way his brain works. If I went there and saw old French buildings, I bet the first thing I'd think is – there must be amazing cheese around here somewhere!

He wrote that he hangs out at a jazz club called the Red Rhino. He met a Vietnamese-Finnish woman there who's working on a book about food traditions that were lost during the war years. He told her what I've been writing about, and she wants me to help her explain her ideas in English so she can get an American publisher. She can get me a visa through a language school. Can you imagine? Frida in Vietnam?

I saw When Harry Met Sally. I know this is the moment when I get the goofy smile on my face and hop on a plane. Confession: I'm smiling. Confession Deux: I'm considering it. I don't want to put what I'm about to tell you next in writing because that will make it capital-R Real – but deep breath – here I go. Glamorous Lauren Dunne says I have too much personality for The New Yorker. It's not about exclamation marks. Apparently I have a kind of unique enthusiasm she doesn't want to see dampened by the magazine's style. She made it sound like a compliment, but I have a feeling it's her way of letting me down easy. Am I bummed out? Most definitely. It's The New Yorker for crying out loud! I've drowned my sorrows in so much raclette my uniquely enthusiastic pores are oozing Swiss cheese. But I've been thinking. What if Sarajevo and the Ramonas aren't the story I'm supposed to tell? What if that's why I'm having so

much trouble writing my essay? What if my story is waiting for me with Kirby in Vietnam?
Searchingly yours,
Frida

P.S. Bobbie got Merjema's transcripts! She can put the book club money toward tuition and books – everyone agreed that's how they want it spent.

5/25/94

Dear Frida,

I've been sitting on the ferry all morning riding back and forth between Seattle and Bainbridge Island. I like to sit on the deck and let my brain dip and soar like the seagulls. When I'm on the water it makes me feel closer to Bumpa.

I brought all of your letters with me. It's taken almost three coffees to read them start to finish. It's so weird we've never met face-to-face. We've been through so much together. I wonder what would have happened in our lives if you had told Kirby to stick it and wrote to your L.A. bookstore for Martha. Or if someone else at my store decided to answer your letter. Can you imagine? It makes me sick thinking about it. I bet I'd still be a brain-jittering insecure mess without you and your renegade exclamation marks. (My brain still jitters, obviously with all the coffee and because I'm still figuring out life, but at least you've helped me tidy up my insecurities so they're not spilling all over the place.)

Just because you're not <u>New Yorker</u> material doesn't mean this isn't your story. I'd like to share a little something from one of your letters. And I quote: "This is it, Kate – this is <u>MY</u> story."

These are your exact words from Sarajevo. This is most definitely your story, whether or not you go to Vietnam. Are you going to Vietnam? Vietnam! Inquiring minds are dying to know.

I'm getting my footing with Sven gone, even though he's still in my life courtesy of the U.S. Postal Service. The other night I went out for tapas and <u>Four Weddings and a Funeral</u> with Kids Books Josephine, Fiction Section Polly, and Travel Section Jane, and when I got home there were three letters and this postcard:

"There is a difference between missing the past, and longing for the future; we get used to being without the things that have passed away; we never get used to being without the things that have not yet come; we end by ceasing to think of those; we never cease to think of these." – Henry James

It's heartbreaking, Frida. All the "yet to come" we shared is gone. Some days I ache for what could have been so badly I can't stop crying, but I know I did the right thing. I spent Sunday in a book coma rereading <u>A Circle of Quiet</u>. Madeleine constantly searches for the meaning of life, but her search is the polar opposite of Sven's. His arms are crossed tight as a vise over his chest, while her arms are flung open wide. He's already decided on the certainties he's searching for because he needs his suffering to make sense. She's committed to "the unknown and unknowable." He needs answers to everything, but she says, "To define everything is to annihilate much that gives us laughter and joy."

When I finished Madeleine, I got an urge to reread <u>Moon Tiger</u>, too. It feels like I discovered it a lifetime ago. Remember how blown away I was by how Penelope wrote from so many overlapping points of view? Reading it now I can see it wasn't just because I'd never encountered a writing style like that before. It was because I'd never experienced life like that before. Billions of different points of view unlike mine. Billions of different versions of life unlike mine. If Sven needs to have his version, that's his right, but this is my life, so guess what? My version! And what if after I finished reading, my version wanted to decoupage a flower pot? Why? Because doing it made me Genuinely Happy.

I'm tired of feeling conflicted because I like to tear up Martha Stewart magazines and decoupage things. Or frivolous because I'm reading Living a Beautiful Life. Why can't I read Alexandra Stoddard and Thomas Merton and learn about meaning from each of them! Merton wrote, "For we cannot make the best of what we are, if our hearts are always divided between what we are and what we are not." Alexandra wrote, "It takes a commitment to enjoy each day fully." Just because Alexandra wants me to use a pretty checkbook cover to make doing bills more pleasant doesn't make her advice less valuable. Can't I love to sing "Porcupine Pie" and still take life seriously? In my version, the answer is yes! (Do you think exclamation marks are contagious? I think I've caught a case of yours!!)

There's another packet waiting for you at the AmEx office.
Love,
Kate

P.S. Speaking of When Harry Met Sally. I needed a change. I cut my hair short. A lot of people say it makes me look like Meg Ryan.

FRIDA RODRIGUEZ ... EN ROUTE

June 4, 1994
Paris, France

You're flourishing, Fair Kate! If you want to give me any credit, I'll take it, but only if you'll take some credit for what I'm about to tell you. I went to Sarajevo because of Niko, but no matter how I feel about Kirby – and I have a lot of feelings – ha! – I can't go to Vietnam because of him. I know they're not the same people. Not even close. The point is that this isn't about them, this is about me, and I couldn't have seen that without you.

It's true what I wrote in Sarajevo. This IS my story. And not just the story I'm supposed to tell but the story I'm supposed to be living. I hope the universe wants Kirby and me to be together in the future, I really do, but right now I need to be here taking care of the Ramonas. I just wish it wasn't so hard. Every time we think the war can't get any worse, it does. And now there's Rwanda too. Did it make its way through all the news about Kurt Cobain over there? There was a massive candlelight vigil for him here, but I haven't seen anything like that in the streets for the Tutsis. How is that possible? There's always some group or other protesting something here, especially on the Left Bank. I can't wrap my mind around the numbers. What kind of evil bulldozes a church with twenty thousand people hiding inside and then kills anyone who tries to escape with machetes? Two hundred and fifty thousand Rwandans fled to Tanzania. Where are they going to go? If the world doesn't care about white ethnic cleansing in Bosnia, no way is it going to care about black genocide in Africa.

It's affecting the Ramonas. I felt especially helpless when Lejla read about the rape squads recruited to infect Tutsi women with HIV. Systematic rape is used as a weapon in Bosnia too. Irena is still there. All the women in Lejla's life are still there. How do you help people find joy in the face of atrocities like that? How do you help them feel secure? I have to figure this out.

Determinedly,

Frida

From the Other Side

Dear Frida,

Where will my life be once the lilacs have come and gone again? I know the answer now. Bumpa caught pneumonia and had to go into the hospital. They put cots in his room so Mom, Franny, and I could sleep there. When I woke up in the middle of the night, I sat by his bed holding his hand. His skin was thin and papery like petals pressed in a book. He had an oxygen mask, and moisture from his breath condensed on his eyelashes like dew. Mom made sure the nurse parted his hair on the usual side, and even without his teeth in, he looked peaceful.

The next day Dad came back for the meeting with the doctor who explained how Bumpa's body was shutting down. Mom called Great-Aunt Irene and Great-Uncle Paul. When they got there we stood in a circle around Bumpa's bed telling his favorite stories, like the time he was nearly swept off his ship during a typhoon in the South China Sea. He woke up in a maternity ward in Manila because it was the only place that had space for him. That's the point in the story where Bumpa would say, "Golly, I sure was surprised," and his face would get as red as a beet. Have I ever told you how modest he was?

After a while the doctor removed his oxygen mask. His breathing started to slow down. Each puff of air was weaker than the one before it, and the stories dissolved so the only sound was the muted beep of the monitors. Franny and I held hands. Dad put his arm around Mom, and she rested her head on his shoulder. Great-Uncle Paul cried softly. They had been friends since he married Great-Aunt Irene in 1933. She looked so lost. Bumpa was the last of her brothers. Her baby brother.

We watched as Bumpa's spirit filled his body. It felt like it stayed inside him forever making sure it wasn't leaving anything behind. But it wasn't forever. He exhaled a long frayed breath, and his body sank into the bed. Dad prayed, thanking God for giving us a man like Bumpa. My thoughts felt thin and clear. A man like Bumpa was <u>my</u> Bumpa. I've never felt so fortunate in my whole life.

There are so many cruel deaths in this world, Frida. Maybe the cruelty is what makes them so hard to fathom. It's a wonder this poor planet doesn't crumble with grief. I thought Bumpa's stroke would make his death cruel. I wish he never had it. I wish I could have learned about myself another way. But I get it. That's not how life works. Before you and I started writing letters, I never could have imagined I'd feel blessed about the death of someone I love so much. My heart's shattered, but I could be Sven, and my heart could be broken because Bumpa was just a sailor in a single-wide trailer who lived a life of quiet desperation. Or I can be me, and my heart can be broken because I lost a man who lived a life of quiet consequence.

I don't know what happened in Chicago, but I do know he came back to us. And he taught me how to love just by being who he was. By always having our favorite black licorice in the candy dish and stopping for maple bars Every Single Time he drove across the state to visit because he knew they made us happy. Bumpa lived his love for us. Like Mom helping him with the jigsaw puzzle at the nursing home. She was living her love for him. You're like Bumpa, Frida. Madeleine L'Engle wrote, "It is the tiny, particular acts of love and joy which are going to swing the balance." Remember when you bought me that Wallace Stegner novel? And the candied lilacs? It's not easy since I cut my hair, but I'm wearing the scrunchie you made me right now. I know exactly how you're going to help the Ramonas find joy and feel secure. One tiny, particular bedtime story, and one tiny, particular spoonful of bosanski lonac, and a million more tiny, particular acts of love at a time.

Love,

Kate

FRIDA RODRIGUEZ ... EN ROUTE

June 24, 1994
Paris, France

Dear Kate,

Every person in this messed-up world should love and be loved like Bumpa. Everyone should have such a loving death. I remember when he had his stroke. Confession: I was scared it was going to make you bitter. It's easy to be bitter, but you didn't let that happen. I wish I could have met him and told him how grateful I am for his Punkin. I wish we could hear him say golly when you publish your first novel because I know someday you're going to publish a novel that will be the exact book a person needs at a certain time in their life. ~~Please give your family my condolences.~~ I don't like that word. It sounds impersonal. Give them hugs from me and I'm sending you the biggest hug of all plus endless admiration for being strong enough to choose the hardest path during the saddest time. Gratitude.
Love,
Frida

7/10/1994

Dear Frida,

Mom and Dad just left to take Franny to SeaTac, but I wanted to stay a little longer. We came here for the weekend to finally pack up Bumpa's trailer. A couple bought it including the furniture, but we had to get his personal stuff. I knew it was going to hurt, but I didn't know how much all the little things would wipe me out. It's so hard to believe he's never going to make another pot in his Mr. Coffee. Or putter around with a broken radio again.

We played gin at his old Formica table our first night, and it felt wrong being there like that without him. He should have said, "Night Shortcake, night Punkin," when Franny and I went to bed in the little side room like when we were kids. When I woke up in the middle of the night, I should have had to tiptoe in the kitchen because he used to make Mom and Dad take his bedroom and he slept on the couch. I wandered around the living room for a while trying to memorize everything. The big Magnavox we used to watch <u>The Flintstones</u> on. The brass sextant he let Franny and me play with like it was any old toy and not an antique. How can such a small space hold so many memories? It's weird to think about new people making memories here.

When I got to the front window, I saw something move outside. Mom was sitting on the porch. The moonlight was bright, and she was staring at the lilac bush. It looked so plain without its purple flowers. I remembered how Bumpa told me she used to wake up in the middle of the night. I bet she looked almost the same then as she does now. She's still so young, and it hit me while I watched her. For the rest of her life she'll never have a dad again. I can't imagine that.

All that time I spent agonizing about how hurt or guilty Bumpa's stroke made me feel. Frida, I never asked Mom how it made her feel. I mean I know she was sad. Of course she was. Who wouldn't be, and especially his daughter? But she didn't talk about it. Not in the way I thought you were supposed to talk about it. I can't believe I almost let Sven convince me that if someone wasn't talking about life in a Big Serious Way, they weren't thinking about it the right way or maybe even thinking about it at all. How limited is that? I mean, have I ever said a word to Mom about any of the things I write in my letters to you? Like how disorienting life is off the boat. Or the bees buzzing under my skin. As far as she knows, my mind's a jolly fairyland filled with rainbows and kittens.

I felt so ashamed of myself. I went outside and knelt in front of her chair so I could hug her. I said, "I'm sorry your dad died." She shook, and I held her tighter. I've never held her like that before. She's the one who holds me when I cry. I could feel the ridge of bones down her spine. She felt fragile, and I thought about how brave you were writing that letter to your mom. Apologizing for making assumptions about her. I wanted to apologize to Mom like that, but my throat started filling with cement. Then I heard you, Frida. As clear as if you were standing right there. You told me to tell her what was in my heart, and you promised me everything would be okay. I said, "I'm sorry I never asked you how Bumpa's stroke made you feel."

She looked up at me. I sat back, and she wiped her tears with her sleeve. She said, "I suppose your dad and I didn't do a great job teaching you girls how to do that." That caught me by surprise, and before I could ask what she meant, she told me how while she was cleaning out Bumpa's desk, she was thinking about things she wished she'd tried to talk to him about. Like when he went to Chicago. She told me when she was growing up, she was Bumpa's whole world, but she didn't realize it. She was only eighteen when she got married and twenty when she had me. She and Dad were starting their own life, doing their own thing. She said, "We didn't know how to ask your Bumpa how he felt when I moved out. We didn't know about depression back then. People didn't talk about things like that. When he came back from Chicago, I didn't know what to say to him."

She brushed a strand of hair off my cheek. I remembered how she did the same thing for Bumpa in the nursing home. I thought about how she was touching me with the same fingers that helped him put the puzzle pieces in the right places. I had so many questions, but her eyes were puffy from crying. She looked completely drained. I asked if she wanted to go to bed. She shook her head and said, "I want to keep talking, kiddo." I love it when she calls me kiddo. I went inside and brewed one more last pot in Bumpa's old coffee maker, and when I came back out, she pulled another chair right up to hers. I tucked my feet up on her lap and said, "It sure is nice to be awake with someone else when the rest of the world is asleep." She smiled and whispered, "Oh, Bumpa."

We talked, Frida. About everything. Old Sven. The boat. Neil Diamond. We were still talking when the sun came up.

Love,

Kate

FRIDA RODRIGUEZ ... EN ROUTE

July 28, 1994
Paris, France

Fair Kate,

I cried when I read your letter. It must be agonizing for moms to wait for their children to finally realize they're Human Beings. We're lucky. Our Human Beings are turning out to be better than we ever could have expected. I finally took your advice and sent my writing to Mom. After she finished freaking out about the library fire and what happened to Branka, she did the most amazing thing. She called her cookbook editor at Random House in New York. Then she sent her some of my pages. The result? Mary Ward-Porter LOVES what I'm doing. She says I definitely have a book and even better, the most appealing part of said book is Me-Myself-I. She says I'm original and universal which is apparently a dream combo for a writer!

I have so much work ahead of me figuring out what I want to say. I know it will be about Sarajevo and Smurfette and growing up and spreading joy. You'll need to help me corral it since every time I turn around, something new happens that I want to write about. Like Mom's last letter. She said she wishes she could let herself into her writing the way I do, but when she tries she feels herself resisting because school drilled it into her that the journalist is never part of the story – then she asked if I'll help her try to write something more personal!

MY editor suggested the title <u>Life in Flight</u>. Can't you see it in a big stack at The Puget Sound Book Company? <u>Life in Flight</u> by Immy Frida Rodriguez. I'm considering using my full name. What do you think?

Blissfully yours,

Frida

From my beloved Ballard burrow

8/14/94

Dear Frida,

I'm over the moon for you. <u>Life in Flight</u>! How can I help? Tell me what you need. Opinions? I have plenty of those, beginning with this one. You better not downplay yourself in this book. You are your story, Frida. You're like Holly in <u>Happy All the Time</u>. "She fought to keep the ugly, chaotic world at bay and to keep a sweet, pretty corner to live in." People need to know that they don't have to fix acid rain or cure cancer to still make a difference in someone's life.

Speaking of asking for help. Are you ready for it? I'm three chapters into writing a new novel. Last week I dug out the one that didn't get published and read it again. What a difference a few years make. It's so obvious to me now what was wrong with it. I thought it should be about my character getting to the place where she learned everything she was supposed to learn. Like there was an actual psychological destination she had to reach before she could start her real life. But that cheesy saying on t-shirts really is true, isn't it? The journey is the destination. Frida, I'm never going to learn everything I need to learn, but that's not the point. The point is to never stop learning and never expect to

KATE & FRIDA

know everything you think you need to know. It's hard to explain, but realizing that made me feel free. Like I can do anything. Run my own bookstore. Hop a plane tonight for Paris. Join you in Vietnam if you ever decide to go. How exciting would that be to have an adventure together in Asia of all places?

Now that Mom and I are into Big Talks, it's like we can't stop. She even bought me one of those three-way phones at Radio Shack so Franny can join in. We've had some intense moments, but every time afterward I feel better than before. Dad gets uncomfortable when the conversation gets too personal (female), so Mom fills him in later. Don't worry. We still play gin rummy and dance to "Sweet Caroline."

Love,
Kate

P.S. How cool is this coincidence? My mom had an aunt named Immy. It's a great name, but I vote for Frida Rodriguez. That's who you are.

FRIDA RODRIGUEZ ... ~~EN ROUTE~~ *Arrived*

August 25, 1994
Paris, France

Fair Kate,

Vietnam together – that would be wild. The two of us running around eating bánh mì and writing our books. Maybe someday – unless – Confession: I did something I hope I don't regret. In my last letter to Kirby I mentioned that maybe I'm in love with him but I won't say for sure until he tells me how he feels and if he isn't in love with me back then he should pretend I never brought it up. It will be a while before I get a response. Letters have to go through some kind of social evils censorship process over there. Kirby jokes that Communism makes him appreciate French bureaucracy. It could take up to a month for my letter to get through to him and another month for his reply to get through to me. Now I know what all those bees buzzing around inside you feels like!

What you wrote a few letters back about tiny, particular acts of love – your words are sinking in, Kate. It's been hard for me to accept that I won't be breaking any glass ceilings. But I'm good at the little things I do. And I like doing the little things. Not just making stew and scrunchies. Now that I have the database up and running, I was surprised to see that I've written tiny, particular letters to sixty-eight university newspapers. Thirty-two have published articles about the project. Not only are people sending books for Bobbie and other journos to take into Sarajevo, a few are offering to sponsor students to come study in the U.S. Small acts really do add up, don't they?

We've come a long way, baby. I can't wait to read your chapters whenever you're ready. I hope you're writing a novel about a family that lives on a boat because I have some thoughts on that. Maybe your metaphorically seafaring family didn't teach you about Tolstoy, Fair Kate, but they did give you kindness and curiosity. You can pick up old Leo anywhere along your Destination Journey, but if you don't get those other things in early – I think they're harder to cultivate the older you get. I'm not sure how you can fit that in or if you even want to. It was just an idea – I have more if you want them! But I'll only send them if you promise to keep sending me yours for my book.

Have an amazing day!

Frida

9/17/94

Dear Frida,

I'm sure you're wondering why this letter wasn't mailed to you. You're wondering why Faith gave it to you and why she made you come to Chez Lisette to read it. What surprise do I have in store for you? Are the Ramonas going to pop out of the kitchen and do a choreographed dance to Fair Kate's Friends Forever Mixtape for Frida?

Be patient. It's a virtue. Not necessarily yours. Ha!

I want to tell you a story.

One sunny summer morning in Seattle, Fair Kate the Bookseller bought an <u>Access Guide to Paris</u> with her employee discount at The Puget Sound Book Company. Then she walked up the street to Metsker Maps to get her passport photo taken before heading to Queen Anne Travel for a round-trip ticket to Paris on TWA.

She packed a suitcase with Émile Zola's <u>The Belly of Paris</u>, Elizabeth Bowen's <u>The House in Paris</u>, and Simone de Beauvoir's <u>The Mandarins</u>. For the non-Paris tasting menu, she chose <u>Corelli's Mandolin</u> (lots of book clubs are reading it even though it's still in hardback) and <u>When Heaven and Earth Changed</u>

<u>Places</u> (so you can learn more about Vietnam). Also crammed in were a Pretenders t-shirt for Lejla, hot-pink Chuck Taylors for Merjema, local goodies (Almond Roca and MarketSpice tea) for Faith and the rest of the Ramonas, two Smurfette outfits for Branka, and boxes of orange Jell-O, Betty Crocker yellow cake mix, and Skippy so I can make Jell-O salad and peanut butter cookies in Lisette's kitchen. (No need to pack butter for making Laurie Colwin's tomato pie crust since you're swimming in it over there.)

When I was rereading your letters on the ferry a while ago, I started making a list of subjects for us to discuss because I knew in my heart we'd meet one day soon. I want to know what you meant when you said color is everything in America, and I have thoughts on why the world can mourn Kurt Cobain but not hundreds of thousands of Tutsis. I typed up four chapters of my novel for you to read (yes, there's a girl playing cards with her dad in the middle of the night), and I've started a notebook of ideas for your book.

Then there is the fat envelope I put in my fanny pack. When everyone at the store found out I was going to Paris, I got called upstairs to the receiving department. The whole gang was there: Stella, Kids Books Josephine, Fiction Section Polly, Travel Section Jane, Caftan Dawn, Special Orders Mae, Night Manager K2, Birkenstock Otis, and of course Roy. They gave me the envelope with these words written on it: "Well done, Perky! Have a nice day!" It contained $2,700 for the Ramona Club!! We get tiny profit-sharing checks every year, and even though the store's owner is always bugging us to buy stock in Microsoft (I guess because it's local), they figured this was a better investment. When Roy hugged me, he slipped a twenty into my pocket and whispered, "Have a Pernod with the ghost of Fitzgerald at Les Deux Magots for me."

By now your clever brain has figured it out.

Look up, Frida.

Look around until you notice the blonde with the shaggy Meg Ryan haircut at the table by the window. Do a double take. Don't just sit there looking stunned. Get over here and give me a hug!

Love from Paris,

Your Fair Friend Kate

Author's Note

Just as Frida and Kate wrote from their hearts to one another, I wrote this novel from my heart to my younger self. The self I was in my early twenties during the early 1990s, working at the Elliott Bay Book Company in Seattle, living on my own for the very first time in a little brick-walled loft apartment, devouring books I'd never heard of before, and making Laurie Colwin's tomato pie. Discovering the world. Discovering my place in the world.

While this is a work of fiction, much in this book was inspired by my own life.

There was a Sven, brilliant and promising, who changed my life. He died tragically at forty-one of the disease that haunted him, with his song still inside him. There was a Roy as emotionally generous as I have described. He also died young, a cruel reminder of the universe's persistent unfairness. There was an unpublished post-college novel and an existential crisis—not that I knew what it was called back then. There was a cozy metaphorical boat that I lived on in great happiness and safety all of my childhood. With a sister who was (and is) my best friend. With a mom who sparked my love of reading with *Miss Twiggley's Tree*. With a dad who took us on special daughter days to Seahawks games and the bookstore where I would work one day. And there was a Bumpa and a stroke and a death that devasted me because my Bumpa was a finer man than any character I could ever write. A man of grace, humility, generosity, and love so genuine and un-wavering it makes me ache wanting just one more day with him.

Along with these facts, there are truths, and that is what I wanted to share with my younger self. I wanted her to know: You won't be confused and lost forever. It was not a waste of time lov-ing someone you outgrew. Growing apart from friends because you live different kinds of lives doesn't mean growing away from your heart's connection to them. You will recover from the grief that dismantled you when Bumpa had his stroke. You will con-tinue to get things wrong, and that's okay. Unlike Kate and Frida, in real life I learned these things gradually, through the many periods of growing up that a person experiences during a lifetime.

While many of Kate's experiences mirror my own, I also shared a kinship with Frida and her desire for a big adventure. To be a foreign war correspondent. Or a spy. Or at least Kelly Gar-rett or some cool modern version of Nancy Drew. Alas, I'm a chicken—bock, bock, bock, as Frida would say. But I did move to Saigon when I left the bookstore in an effort to expand my view of the world. If I could have set Frida there I would have, but in the early 1990s, she and Kate could not have exchanged books and letters freely in and out of Communist Vietnam. So I chose romantic, enchanting Paris, which turned out to be a per-fect location, unfolding Frida's story into Sarajevo.

AUTHOR'S NOTE

I have not been in a war, but my time in Vietnam—entrusted with the life stories of close Vietnamese friends during the four years I lived there and the decades since—taught me that war can shatter an individual's sense of self and disfigure a society. I hoped to honor what I learned about the never-ending struggle to overcome loss and reconstruct identity through Frida's experience in Sarajevo, a conflict that I still find incomprehensible and despicable, as all wars are. Taking place at the end of the twentieth century, the 1,425-day Siege of Sarajevo was the longest siege in modern European history. Serb forces artillery, including an average of 329 mortar shells per day, destroyed the National Library just as I described—an act of culturicide that is said to be the largest single book burning in history. Those weapons also killed an estimated 11,540 people in the city, including more than 500 children.

One of those children was Amel Hodžić. I connected with his younger brother, Džemil, through his website Sniper Alley in the course of doing my research. As I asked Džemil questions, I learned the story of Amel. Toward the end of the war, during a so-called ceasefire, the boys were outside. Amel was playing tennis while Džemil played marbles with his friends. A sniper started shooting, and Amel was shot in the chest. In the words of Džemil, who was twelve at the time: "I phoned the ambulance and went out to witness what would be the last moments of my brother. He died on my mother's lap while she tried her best to bring him back to life."

Back when I was in my early twenties, I could not grasp how it was acceptable to be happy when such suffering existed in the world. In my fifties, as I was writing *Kate & Frida*, the world had not changed. Children are still dying in wars, and each one is a reason that we must, with all our hearts, find ways to keep joy alive.

As Mary Oliver wrote: "Joy is not made to be a crumb."

This, especially, in writing *Kate & Frida*, is what I wanted my younger self to know: During the darkest times, not only is it possible to feel joy, it is your duty to embrace it fully, to share it far and wide, and to never lose hope that joy, along with compassion and love, will win in the end.

Recipes

MY MOM'S
PEANUT BUTTER COOKIES

Cookie making with our mom is a memory my sister and I treasure. Especially snickerdoodles and these peanut butter cookies. The best thing about this recipe is how easy it is for a child to make on their own . . . my own experience excluded! When I was ten or eleven, on my first solo attempt (not only at cookie making, but at cooking altogether), I used a cup of water instead of a tablespoon. Mom, being the best kind of mom there is, poured the batter into a loaf pan and called the result peanut butter bread. Was it any good? Probably not, but my dad and uncles ate it enthusiastically. Below is the version that has been in my recipe book for years, although I have a feeling that somewhere along the line I re-typed it, exchanging shortening for vegetable oil. Yes, there was a time when my cupboard always contained Crisco!

1 package yellow cake mix (extra moist)
1 cup peanut butter (Skippy is best)
½ cup vegetable oil

1 tablespoon water

2 eggs

Combine ingredients and drop in 1-inch-or-so balls onto un-greased cookie sheet. Press a crisscross pattern on the top of each cookie with a fork. Bake at 350°F for 12 minutes.

Makes about 24 cookies

FRIDA'S MOM'S
CHILES RELLENOS DE QUESO

This recipe comes from Mexican Cookery *by Barbara Hansen, who was the inspiration for Frida's mom, Joan, from* Love & Saffron. *It's a recipe of its time (the 1970s), using substitutions for ingredients that weren't as commonly available then as they are now—but that's part of the fun. Just imagine Frida making this dish for the Ramonas in the bistro kitchen in Paris, and I hope you enjoy it as much as they did. As for the best chiles to use, Barbara's use of "California chiles" refers to the Anaheim chile, while poblano chiles are most common for this dish.*

Tomato sauce (see below)

6 California chiles, roasted, peeled, or 6 canned whole green chiles

4 ounces Monterey Jack cheese

Oil for frying

3 eggs, separated

About ½ cup all-purpose flour

TOMATO SAUCE

4 small tomatoes, peeled (1 lb.)

½ medium onion or 1 small onion (yellow or white)

1 garlic clove

1 tablespoon vegetable oil

½ cup chicken broth

½ teaspoon salt

2 small California chiles, peeled, seeded, chopped, or ¼ cup
  canned chopped green chiles

Pinch ground cloves

Pinch ground cinnamon

FOR THE CHILES

1. Prepare tomato sauce (see next page); keep warm.
2. Cut as small a slit as possible in one side of each chile to remove the seeds. Leave on stems. Pat chiles dry with paper
   towels.
3. Cut cheese into 6 long thin sticks. Place 1 stick in each chile.
   Use more cheese if chiles are large. If chiles are loose and
   open, wrap around cheese and fasten with wooden picks.
4. Pour oil ¼-inch deep into a large skillet. Heat oil to 365°F.
5. Beat egg whites in a medium bowl until stiff. Slightly beat egg

yolks in a small bowl. Add all at once to beaten egg whites. Fold in lightly but thoroughly.

6. Roll chiles in flour, then dip in egg mixture to coat.
7. Fry in hot oil until golden brown, turning with a spatula. Drain on paper towels.
8. Top with tomato sauce and serve immediately.

Makes 6 servings

FOR THE TOMATO SAUCE

1. Combine tomatoes, onion, and garlic in blender or food processor; puree.
2. Heat oil over medium heat in a medium saucepan. Add tomato mixture. Cook 10 minutes, stirring occasionally.
3. Add broth, salt, chiles, cloves, and cinnamon. Simmer gently 15 minutes.

Makes about 2 cups

BALKAN LUNCH BOX BOSANSKI LONAC

This is the first dish that Frida makes for Lejla on a hot plate in her small Paris hotel room, to offer her solace and a taste of home when she is far from Sarajevo. I chose it because it's considered both a national dish of Bosnia and comfort food. Many thanks to Aida Ibišević and Aleksandra Jaha for sharing this recipe with readers of Kate & Frida. *On their mouthwatering website Balkan Lunch Box, you will find the history of this dish, instructional photos, FAQs, and optional additional ingredients, as well as numerous other recipes from the Balkans.*

MEAT

2 to 4 pounds of two, preferably three, types of meat (fatter cuts) such as mutton, lamb, and beef; beef and mutton; lamb and beef; beef and pork; or veal and beef. If you have only one type of meat, choose two different cuts like rib and chuck, shank and flank, etc. Chunk the meat.

VEGETABLES

1 cabbage head (green) smaller, cut into 8 to 10 pieces

1 to 2 yellow onions, quartered

3 to 4 whole garlic cloves, peeled

3 large carrots, peeled and diced

8 ounces green or yellow beans cut into 1-inch pieces

4 ounces peas

3 to 4 large potatoes (Russet or yellow), peeled and diced

3 to 4 large tomatoes, skinned, and diced, or an 8-ounce can

2 to 3 bell peppers, cut into chunks

HERBS AND SEASONINGS

1 teaspoon salt

1 teaspoon ground black peppercorns

3 to 4 strands of parsley whole or about 1 cup chopped
1 teaspoon paprika
1 to 2 tablespoons stock powder or Vegeta, or 1 bouillon cube, crushed

1. Choose a clay pot, ceramic pot, Dutch oven, or regular cooking pot. Layer the ingredients into your pot one by one (keep the meat on the bottom). Add the blend of seasonings in between layers. Add just enough water (or water and tomato sauce) to touch the vegetables on top, but not to cover them completely.
2. Cover the pot. If you don't have a lid, use parchment paper and twine, tying the twine around the top of the pot to secure the paper like a lid.
3. Choose a cooking method based on your pot. If cooking in a clay pot, ceramic pot, or Dutch oven, transfer the pot to the oven. Cook at 350°F for about 3 hours. If cooking in a regular pot, cook it on the stovetop on low for about 3 hours. Don't remove the lid or parchment paper during cooking, and the stew should not be stirred.
4. Serve the stew warm or store by letting it cool down completely, then transferring to the fridge for up to 3 days. The stew is best 1 to 2 days after it's made. Reheat on the stovetop on low. Add ½ cup of water if necessary.

Serves 4–6

LAURIE COLWIN'S TOMATO PIE

When I was in my early twenties, I made Laurie Colwin's Tomato Pie recipe from More Home Cooking *more times than I can count. It was my first "adult" recipe. My first invite-friends-over-for-lunch dish. It's impossible to express how thrilled I am to share it. I'm extremely grateful to Laurie's child, RF Jurjevics, for their generosity in allowing me this honor.*

Most of Laurie's recipes in Home Cooking *and* More Home Cooking *were written directly into the prose as part of narrative essays. I am listing out the ingredients here for convenience so they can be prepared in advance, before sharing the recipe as is in Laurie's own words. The Mary she refers to is her friend Mary O'Brien, who gave her this recipe.*

DOUBLE BISCUIT-DOUGH CRUST

2 cups flour

1 stick butter

4 teaspoons baking powder

Approx. ¾ cup milk (or I like to use buttermilk)

FILLING

Two 28-ounce cans plum tomatoes, drained and thinly sliced

Chopped basil, chives, or scallions

1½ cups sharp Cheddar, grated
⅓ cup mayonnaise thinned with 2 tablespoons lemon juice

The pie has a double biscuit-dough crust, made by blending 2 cups flour, 1 stick butter, 4 teaspoons baking powder, and approximately ¾ cup milk, either by hand or in a food processor. You roll out half the dough on a floured surface and line a 9-inch pie plate with it. Then you add the tomatoes. Mary makes this pie year round and uses first-quality canned tomatoes, but at this time of year 2 pounds of peeled fresh tomatoes are fine, too. Drain well and slice thin two 28-ounce cans plum tomatoes, then lay the slices over the crust and scatter them with chopped basil, chives, or scallions, depending on their availability and your mood. Grate 1½ cups sharp Cheddar and sprinkle 1 cup of it on top of the tomatoes. Then over this drizzle ⅓ cup mayonnaise that has been thinned with 2 tablespoons lemon juice, and top everything with the rest of the grated Cheddar. Roll out the remaining dough, fit it over the filling, and pinch the edges of the dough together to seal them. Cut several steam vents in the top crust and bake the pie at 400°F for about 25 minutes. The secret of this pie, according to Mary, is to reheat it before serving, which among other things ensures that the cheese is soft and gooey. She usually bakes it early in the morning, then reheats it in the evening in a 350°F oven until it is hot.

Serves 6

Acknowledgments

For *Kate & Frida*, I offer my gratitude:

To the Elliott Bay Book Company for being my chrysalis and exhilarating book playground for five of the most formative years of my life. You guided me toward the sweet spot between who I was and who I wanted to become. Along with giving me a Sven to help me grow and Roy to soothe my buzzing bees with his calm joy, you gave me one of my dearest friends in all the world, Beth (Stella); my letter-writing soulmate Janet (Kids Books Josephine); my book, book, book friend Kurtis (Otis), who was hired the same day I was as a holiday gift wrapper; mentors Kristin (K2) and Kay (Mae), whose trust in me helped me trust myself; and a cast of characters no Austen, Wharton, or Trollope novel of manners could ever compete with: Holly (Fiction Section Polly), Joan (Travel Section Jane), Jill, Deanna and Tim, Mike, Steve, Bruce, Robert and Patty, Kristin A., Kristy, Hannah, Barbara, Chris H., Jeff, Tracy and Greg, Margaret and Steven, Joel, Jesse, Erica, Mark, Gordon, Michael, Jutta, Bernie, John M., John H., Kit/Chris D., Janet K., Melanie, Robert L., Rick, and Maggie and Walter. Under your wings made of tens of thousands of books, I experienced learning curves, wake-up calls, and so much magic including those late-night literature-laden gossip sessions (Roy, I miss you so), the unforgettable "I Feel Pretty" party, marathon after-hours Hearts games, the chance to fangirl with Cees Nooteboom (much to his confusion), dressing up like Dorothy Parker to see *Mrs. Parker and the Vicious Circle*, and a very sentimental education.

To the books and authors mentioned in this novel. I was so wide-eyed as a reader when I arrived at Elliott Bay that British fiction was "exotic" to me. Anything beyond that blew my jittering mind. I kept a reading journal during those days, and I wish I could have included every book in it—*God's Snake*, *Miles from Nowhere*, *Rumors of Peace*, *Jazz*, *The Camomile Lawn*, *The Sheltering Sky*, *Final Payments* . . . to all the books mentioned and those I couldn't fit in, you educated me, you inspired me, and you deserve immortality. Merci! (And an apology to any books whose publication dates I shifted for my own poetic license.)

To the Los Angeles and Seattle Public Libraries for their access to newspaper archives that were essential to my research, and to my beloved guidebooks from the 1990s: *Seattle's Best Places*, *Paris Access*, and Patricia Wells's *The Food Lover's Guide to Paris*.

To Kate Garrick. You are my emotional support agent and so much more. Your generosity, practicality, sense of humor, and wisdom make you an extraordinary agent and an even finer human being.

To Tara Singh Carlson. I thought I was the luckiest author in the world when you edited *Love & Saffron*, but my esteem soared to new heights with *Kate & Frida*. Not only are you insightful, enthusiastic, and fair, you understand how to help me stay true to my heart.

To my team at Putnam, thank you Aranya Jain, Molly Donovan, Madeline Hopkins, Leah Marsh, Kristen Bianco, and Shina Patel for making the publishing process such a smooth one. And thank you, Madeline Hopkins, for your care and helping me wrangle Frida's crazy syntax and punctuation.

To Lynn Buckley for this gorgeous cover design (I want this painting for my wall!), and to my bighearted friend Christie Kwan for once again capturing the spirit of my novel in her illustrations.

To Džemil Hodžić of Sniper Alley, who helped me understand Sarajevo during the siege. The conflict was an incredibly complex tangle of ethnicity, nationality, and religion, and any errors in this novel are mine and mine alone.

To Aida Ibišević and Aleksandra Jaha of Balkan Lunch Box for sharing the beauty of Bosnian food and explaining the flavors and ingredients that make Bosnian dishes unique within the larger picture of Balkan cuisine.

To my supportive early *Kate & Frida* readers Anitra Ralph, Jen Bergmark, Cheryl Crocker McKeon, Katrina Woolford, and Stephanie Santos. And to Désirée Zamorano for sharing your Paris years with me and allowing me to give those to Frida, who especially loved those hot dogs wrapped in melted Gruyère.

To the Dorland Mountain Arts Colony and my generous friend Sarah Spearing. As I entered the home stretch in this novel, you gave me the invaluable gift of quiet spaces to write without interruption.

To Huong Nguyen Petkoska. My little sister, my Piglet, a child of war and loss—you inspire me by not only bringing luminous joy and kindness wherever you go, but also by being intentional with Kristijan in the way you are raising your beautiful daughter Elena to bring joy into the world.

To Dad. Could there be a better dad in the universe than the one who raised Julie and me? No! You made us laugh until our stomachs ached with Raggedy Kojak, and you still make us feel safe in the world. You have supported our dreams with encouragement, and you have taught us how to live by the example of your hard work, integrity, irrepressible smile, and unwavering love.

To Mom. Beyond giving us a loving, safe, and endlessly fun childhood with the prettiest, kindest, and (when necessary) fiercest mom around, you encouraged me to grow, allowed me space to grow, and grew along with me, just as Kate and her mom do in this novel. It's an honor to be your daughter, and it was an honor to sit with you and Julie and work together on scenes in this book, sharing beautiful memories and remembering how fortunate we are.

To Julie. My dancing girl-lobster-butterfly, *Love Story*–loving, Leaf Jr. little sis—you are Frida. No matter how hard life gets or hopeless it feels, you always make time and space for tiny, particular acts of love and joy to lift others up. As a sister. As a daughter. As a mom to one-of-a-kind Oliver and lovely Charlie. As a nana to precious Beau. As a friend, as well as a stranger to those you encounter throughout your days. You are my role model for spreading joy and making others feel special.

To Jim. This part of our journey was particularly meaningful as we embraced creativity together—you with your album *Love and Fate* and me with this novel *Kate & Frida*. The way you believe in me creates a sanctuary where I feel free to chase my dreams. Once again, long live tiny wine, dance parties, and our crazy love for one another and Mabel, otherwise known as Barnacle Betty.

To Bumpa. I know that if you were still here to read this book, you would say golly and duck your head and blush at all the praise. That, of course, is what makes you Bumpa. A man of quiet consequence. I love you and miss you every day.